"YOU ORION SCUM," HE SAID, "ALWAYS thinking you can just do whatever you want."

That was decidedly not what I was expecting.

"Oh, I know who you are. Traitor for a father and a piece of filth for a brother."

"My brother?" The words were slow and sluggish in my mouth.

"Worked for him a couple of years back. Wanna see how he rewards his faithful?" The man shifted so that his left hand pressed against my neck while his other hand reached up to unzip his flight suit.

Confusion, angst, fear, trepidation, worry—all that was coursing inside me. I felt like a cloud jumper hocked up on stim-pills. I lifted a leg to try to give him a good swift kick in the tenders, but he managed to hook my leg with a foot and pinned it against the wall.

"This is what my devotion got me," he snarled as he pulled the zipper down to his waist, reached up, and tugged down on the collar of his shirt.

Horrific burns coated his skin—thick, calloused scars of knotted flesh.

He leaned forward. "Tell me why I shouldn't visit the same on his sister."

THE THREE-FOLD SUNS

The Rapscallion
Project Clear Sight

PROJECT CLEAR SIGHT

THE THREE-FOLD SUNS

Book 2

by

ELIZABETH KNOLLSTON

LEWIS BROS PRESS

for all of my aunts and uncles
who have cheered me on
with this wild adventure of mine
thank you
(and the few odd dogs too,
life wouldn't be the same
without you)

1

It's All about the Drama

"Those aren't zips," I protested, eyeing the dubious-looking pastries.

No way in a full burn around Saturn's rings were those certified Zipper-Mates. Honest-to-goodness zips carried the mark of the Old Earth Food Licensing Board baked into the soft, buttery goodness of a zip's outer pastry shell.

The Neetho working that unfortunate food stall waved a tentacle or two and sputtered at me. "Fresh off the *Tur Osho*. Finest fresh-produce transport on this side of Torth's Portals."

"No, they're not," I argued.

The Neetho turned a brilliant shade of crimson as a tentacle snaked forward and snatched the rip-off zips from the counter.

"Trust me. I've learned a lesson or two about certified food. Those aren't zips, and there's no way the *Tur Osho* is a fresh-produce transport. Maybe a waste-fuel transport or a black market—"

"She'll take two," interrupted the man who'd become my shadow.

I turned and glared at Cain. "You know as well as I those aren't certified. No stamp, see?" I pointed at the knockoffs suspended in a display above the counter.

Cain ignored me and my furious gestures. "Exchange the credits."

The sheer amount of willpower necessary to do as instructed was enough to fuel a small colony outpost generator. I gritted my teeth and held my palm over the reader.

"Thank you for your purchase, Kimmi Washlo. Please come again," the automated voice chimed.

If you ever need to move under the radar, let me suggest the HL-359 dermal patch kit. Program the patch with a brand-new identity—feel free to be as detailed as you like—then slap the sucker over your HalfLife biochip. Make sure you wait the full thirty minutes for the patch to absorb. The masking signal will extend out in a two-and-a-half-meter radius to shield the legitimate HalfLife biochip. Once the process is complete, head out on your merry way.

The downfall in that situation was that I didn't get a choice in picking out my false identity. The name Kimmi didn't feel… quite right. But Cain had insisted on keeping a low profile and had slapped on the dermal patch before I could protest. That was a smart play as the patch would make tracing our digital fingerprints difficult while we investigated Project Clear Sight. Then we would go back to business as normal—whatever normal was anymore.

After being trapped on the *Rapscallion* with Mrs. Gol, uncovering the unwanted truth about my father, and realizing someone at Confore Tech wanted me dead, I thought "normal" had taken an abrupt detour completely off the map—not to mention almost dying of a nefarious bacterium my father had used to kill a slew of people and getting tangled up with the notorious Star Eater cult, who inexplicably saved my life and—surprise, surprise—had made some kind of deal with my father. Plus, I'd made my own deal with Cain, my annoying IGJ shadow, in order to figure out what Project Clear Sight really was.

Add that all up, toss in a few onions and some bitter herbs, and I had a life salad chock-full of pure chaos.

Anyway, in the long run, if we were to get the chance to step back into our real lives, that would be the hardest part of all. The mounds of forms and red tape associated with HalfLife identity updates was unimaginable.

"Waste of credits, if you ask me," I muttered as Cain took the proffered zip knockoffs.

"I didn't," Cain replied and handed me a pastry. *<Upsetting every single vendor we go to isn't going to help us in the long run. We're supposed to be blending in. While we're digitally masked, create too big a ruckus, and some enterprising fool may get it in their head to do a little research.>*

I snatched the offending all-in-one meal, took a sniff, and made a face. That earned a rather nasty look from Cain as he unzipped the transparent pouch on his own zip and took a big bite.

<Blending in doesn't mean we have to eat garbage.> I held the foul-smelling piece of food at arm's length, marched

over to a waste can, turned to stare directly at Cain, and dropped the zip in the trash.

His response was to take another big bite and slowly chew with a malicious grin.

"I'd dump you in the waste can if I could," I grumbled.

The stench of the zip reminded me of the foul mess we'd landed in—a big, miserable smelly snag in the fabric of our best-laid plans. We hadn't made it to Lunar 5. That little picnic excursion Mrs. Gol had whipped up for me triggered a cascading effect through the more civilized regions of settled space.

Cain didn't receive a resounding round of applause from the IGJ nor a bump in rating for making sure I lived through tour time on the *Rapscallion*. Let's just say he wasn't in the top-ten list for agents angling for the employee-of-the-month award. Cain had received a clear message to cease and desist, turn over any and all case files, recordings, or evidence, and report in—a cut-and-dried way of saying the whole debacle with Mrs. Gol and her secret chamber of horrors had been neatly tossed out the air lock.

Suffice it to say, our names were popping up on the IGJ's pesky little watch list.

But being on the watch list wasn't a no-no for the upstanding citizens of Lunar 5. The base wasn't known for its welcoming attitude toward the IGJ or its agents. That attitude was due, in large part, to the founding family's ravenous appetites for black market goodies, which translated into an ongoing game of tag for transport and cargo ships in and out of Lunar 5 controlled space.

What we needed was either a planet's worth of credits

to pay the exorbitant rates for a smuggler or our own way past IGJ checkpoints at Lunar 5.

Cain had tried to book passage on a few freighters and even a personal taxi service, but all the deals had fallen through at the last minute. With limited options, we were forced to lie low on Epsilon's Station for far longer than either one of us liked.

The station was a free-floating piece of junk, under the control of the Little Asteroid Gang. Don't let the name fool you—it's not a cutesy kid's science club. Those pesky assassins from the *Starshine*, players with the Tretoono Club, are the elite of the elite when it comes to that line of work. The Little Asteroid Gang is a close second.

Every day, I thank my lucky stars Cain and I are still alive—not just because of recent events, but despite the less-than-stellar company of Epsilon's Station, the Tretoono Club wouldn't send a pair of goons for revenge, risking all-out war by overstepping into Little Asteroid territory.

My best guess is our little victory against the Tretoono assassins scored us at least a few points with the Little Asteroids. Maybe it wasn't enough to be added to the birthday-and-holiday-best-wishes list, but no one had hassled us. Realistically, though, the Little Asteroids were probably trying to figure out how to score a win against the Tretoono Club and make bank off us.

In summary, we were stuck on Epsilon's Station in the meantime. That meant putting up with junky meals and even junkier lodgings.

We passed another Neetho vendor. It waved its

tentacles at me and turned crimson. *Great. Now, I'm on the Neetho hive mind watch list.*

<*See, my point: you're attracting too much attention,*> Cain said telepathically.

<*I thought that was the point of our little scenario. Which, by the way—I'm still not happy I'm bait… again.*>

<*If we want off this station, this is the way it plays out. Is he watching?*>

<*Well, I'm not exactly going to swing my head around and make a point of looking for him, am I?*> I let my irritation leak through our telepathic connection, quite sure Cain was getting the message loud and clear.

"Heard anything yet?" I asked, changing the subject.

"No," Cain replied.

"I'll take the longer answer for a thousand, please."

"No, I haven't heard anything yet, and it's been twenty minutes since I last checked channels," Cain said.

I ground my teeth. Despite Cain's low-ranking and unpopular status, he still had access to IGJ channels. Without fresh information, we were wasting fuel.

We needed a win—namely, to unravel the mysteries of the IGJ case dubbed Project Clear Sight. We knew that Jorge had been the IGJ agent plant within Confore Tech and that, out of the blue, he'd stopped reporting in—no warnings, no hint of double-dealing, nothing. Then his body turned up on Lunar 5 with no leads as to why he'd traveled all the way to that particular lunar base and no hints of foul play. If we could ever get off that junk-heap station, we could've started our little investigation and figured out what got Jorge killed and what in the worlds that had to do with me.

I would really have liked to understand why someone wanted me dead. I would assume most people would want to understand why a contract was put out on them, and if they wouldn't... well, maybe they're a little too invested in the criminal underworld and that's all in a normal day.

I'm not judging, mind you.

Cain needed answers to boost his bottomed-out ranking with the IGJ. If the I'm Going to Keep Everything to Myself Man earned back some respect and gained the proper clearance, Cain would be able to open a fresh case to investigate the wrongful imprisonment of his sister on Dar.

"I can hear you when you're sulking," Cain said. *<And so can anyone else who might be able to listen in. We've got to make this believable.>*

"So?" I grumbled.

Cain popped the last of the zip in his mouth and chewed with malicious purpose before he answered. "It's hard to think when you're constantly projecting your insecurities."

"Excuse me?" I stopped and turned to stare at the man.

Cain returned my scrutinizing look. His emerald eyes glowed with thinly veiled disgust. His feline-esque tail twitched back and forth, and I couldn't help but feel the need to stomp on it.

Saturn's rings, why were his eyes going emerald... again? I wasn't projecting my insecurities but merely considering our options. At least they weren't pitch black. Then I would consider running or hiding behind something. No, scratch that, running would be a much better option.

"I can't take much more of this," Cain snapped. "You're always in my way. I can't think or figure out a plan because you're underfoot. Either physically or mentally."

"If you think you can do better, Mr. Holier Than Thou, by all means, go ahead," I all but shouted.

"You know, I think I will," he retorted. But before I turned and stomped back the way we'd come, Cain's eyes flashed with a hint of amber. *<Be careful.>*

2

The Self-proclaimed Madman

Epsilon's Station's vendor row was crammed with a variety of species that tried to hock their ill-gotten wares on the unlucky few who ventured through the credit death traps. Unfortunately, I had earned quite the reputation, and most of the vendors ignored me as I stalked past the goods, all for "bargain" prices.

I turned down a narrow access corridor, a shortcut back to the lifts. At least, it would have been if not for a bulky, armor-plated Shilo-Torp blocking my way. He was right on cue. Cain and I really were trying to keep a low profile on the station, except where that guy was concerned. We'd been working at keeping his attention fixed on us, according to Cain's plan.

Originally a pacifist species, they'd come from the aquatic world of Shil, but once the Shilo-Torps discovered the lucrative credit flow available in responding to bodyguard and heavy-muscle job listings, the species never looked back. And that particular Shilo-Torp worked for the big bad boss of the station, a man who'd taken a curious interest in me.

So Cain, being the paranoid IGJ agent he was, cooked up a plan, using me as bait—again—to gain a rather unconventional introduction to the boss.

"Finally breaking it off with the *frothli*?" the Shilo-Torp asked. The AI Voca-box that particular Shilo-Torp had the misfortune of having plugged into its vocal cords never ceased to tempt me into fits of giggles. Too bad he didn't have the credits to update to a voice of his own choosing instead of the standard human woman.

"He's not a weak-minded fool... just a stubborn, bull-headed, annoying piece of space junk," I grumbled. "But I take it you saw our little disagreement?"

The Shilo-Torp nodded. "You come with me and make it all better," his AI voice crooned.

I snorted. "Dosing isn't going to solve my problems."

Stunners and stingers were a solid business investment on Epsilon's Station for the right person without a conscience.

"Naw, not talking about dosing. My boss knows you want off this heap of junk, has an offer. Offer for you."

"Tempting. But I'm low on credits right now. I doubt I could afford your boss's price." I threw the Shilo-Torp an apologetic smile as I tried to squeeze by, but his arm shot out and nearly took off my head.

"Hey, watch it, big guy." I rubbed my nose and took a step back.

"You think you find better deal?"

I took a deep breath. That sort of place had no good

deals, hence the ridiculous charade with the Shilo-Torp. "I might."

The Shilo-Torp clicked his beak in what was a no-nonsense response.

"Fine. I'll hear your boss out. But I'm not promising anything, hear me?"

"And the *frothli*?" he asked.

I snorted. "He can find his own way."

The Shilo-Torp grinned, a disconcerting gesture for the species. Biologically, Shilo-Torps didn't have teeth in the human sense of dental design. The Shilo-Torp opened his beak to reveal numerous stalactite-looking structures, which were, in fact, papillae. The papillae lined the inside of the mouth, the esophagus, and even their guts. Evolution had designed the structures to allow the Shilo-Torps to easily grasp and graze on a type of jellyfish-like creature abundant in the Shil oceans.

Dr. Si-Ial Ashter, a preeminent xenologist, had spent several of his early years on Shil. My father made Dr. Ashter's research papers mandatory reading in—

Oh boy. Sorry. I did the whole getting-lost-down-a-wormhole deal again. And I don't feel like talking about my father right now. That's a subject I can't quite stomach at the moment.

While I was mentally meandering down Shilo-Torp Biology 101, I followed the bulbous creature down the access corridor. Soon, we exited at Epsilon's Station's main terminal hub. To the right were the lifts to the higher decks, all mainly hab-units for short- and long-time dwellers, and to the left were checkpoints for the various docking rings.

The Shilo-Torp headed forward, straight to the maintenance and control bunkers. I highly doubted the big guy moonlighted as a part of the station's workforce, not with the abundance of narrow crawl spaces undoubtedly peppered throughout the station. Nor did I think the Shilo-Torp's boss would allow divided loyalties with his employees picking up other jobs, because I did know who his boss was: Miles High.

The man had everyone in his pocket, and his was the palm you had to grease in order to set up shop on Epsilon.

My escort didn't flinch as he walked up to Maintenance Door Nine and waited for the bioscan. A discreet light above the door blinked red then turned a steady green as the door popped open. The Shilo-Torp ducked inside but held the door open and motioned for me to follow.

I knew I should've learned a lesson from the *Rapscallion* about following nefarious individuals into corridors and unknown spaces. But I shrugged, took note of the small locking box jutting out of the lower-left corner of the doorframe, and took aim. Along with a well-timed trip, my hand flew out and landed on the bioscanner. *Gotcha. <Hurry up and follow us inside.>* To my surprise, the Shilo-Torp reached out to help, but I smiled and waved him off.

"Just trying for that grand entrance, you know?" I joked.

Smoothing my jumpsuit and taking a deep breath, I stepped into the dimly lit corridor and into what could only be described as the worst taste in interior design I had ever laid eyes on. I thought the *Starshine* had been garish.

Curtains stained a deep maroon had been draped over the drab gray metallic walls of the station. Gold chains of delicate stars hung over the curtains, and the sky-blue carpeting was so plush that my entire foot sank into its fibrous goodness up to my ankles. I couldn't imagine the cleaning bills the place must rack up.

When the Shilo-Torp clicked his beak, I threw him a dirty look. "I get it. I'm moving, but you should know it's like walking through mud on Talcioush Prime."

After the unexpected workout of moving through a series of convoluted corridors, the shag carpeting gave way to a black-and-white tile-lined floor in a very spacious room.

Rounded platforms stuck out from the walls like fungi on tree trunks, each protrusion sporting a few tables and chairs. In the center of the room was another rounded platform, complete with an old-school band setup. Talk about a throwback to the gangster clubs of Earth's yesteryear.

I wouldn't have expected any less from ex-royalty.

Yup, Miles High was the would-be emperor of Old Earth.

"Speaking of the Farle," I muttered.

Lounging on a platform a few feet off the ground was none other than the big bad boss himself.

"Life extensions looking good, I see." I knew I had a poor habit of taunting those who could easily kill me.

Miles grinned, complete with crimson-stained teeth tucked behind lips permanently dyed black. Just to clear up any possible wrong impressions, Miles High was a lunatic—a very dangerous lunatic.

The man jumped up and vaulted over the platform's railing. "Got the latest bioupgrades from Old Earth. Courtesy of my nephew. Now, there's a man who can't keep his fingers out of the honeypot, if you know what I mean."

Gag. No, I didn't, and no, I didn't want to.

"Muscles here says you might want to cut a deal with me." I pointed at the Shilo-Torp, who hadn't backed up.

"Did he, now?" Miles asked with a sly grin.

"The piece of *frothli* seems to have crossed the line," the Shilo-Torp reported, making me bite my lip to keep from laughing at that blasted female AI voice.

"And what says our little harbinger of death?" Miles inquired.

The laughter died in my chest. I narrowed my eyes and asked, "What did you just call me?"

"Oh, come now, you're on the tip of everyone's tongue—at least those in the know, anyway." Miles had the audacity to wink at me. "The daughter of the infamous Wats Hawking Orion. The ordeal aboard the *Rapscallion.* A contract out on you."

"How do you know about the *Rapscallion?*" I snapped. *Whoops.* "I mean… I don't know who you're talking about. My name is Kimmi—"

"Oh come now, did you think a little old patch would fool the likes of me?" Miles asked in a sickly sweet voice.

I supposed we shouldn't have.

Miles's eyes danced in delight. "Dear, I have ears where no ears should ever be. But they serve their purpose." He twirled back and forth a few times, presumably to the beat of the off-kilter drums in his head, before he leaned against the railing of one of the lower platforms. "But you're not here to discuss your little adventure, are you?"

"No." Since he knew who I was, I saw no point in keeping up the pretense any longer.

"You want off my little station, yes?"

I nodded.

"Rumor is you're trying to find a way to Lunar 5." He leaned forward and asked, "What if I could help you with that? What would you do for me in return?"

"Wait tables for a few nights?" I offered.

Miles roared with laughter. "I think we're going to need to do better than that." He bounced off the railing and bounded over to me. I tried not to grimace as he tucked a strand of my hair behind my ear. "I've got a message that needs sending. But old school like. Not through traceable comms or links."

"Let me guess. A message to Lunar 5."

"Oh, she's a quick one, isn't she?" Miles touched his nose and winked. "So, what do you say? You help me, and I'll help you."

I ground my teeth. We really did need to get off that station.

"Why me? You can't tell me you don't have a handful of goons all eager to jump at a snap of your fingers," I said.

"True. But there's a certain sense of pleasure your presence gives me, knowing how you vanquished a few of my rivals."

I thanked my lucky stars that was where he was headed with his little statement about pleasure.

"Also," the madman continued, "none of my usuals appear to have the connections I need in order to get this little message delivered—connections you seem to have, odd though they may be."

"I don't know who you've been dosing with, but if you really know who we are, then you're talking to the wrong person. I'm not the one with connections. You should've talked with Cain."

A switch flipped inside the crime boss. One moment, Miles was jovial and lighthearted, and the next thing I knew, he was at my throat. Fingers with flamboyant three-inch-long nail art pressed against my neck.

"That miserable piece of scum can crawl back into the hole from which he came," Miles growled. "This offer is only for you."

All righty, then. "Purist much?"

Miles squeezed and glared at me. "No."

I blinked. I wasn't expecting that.

"I wouldn't do business with that traitorous piece of trash if my life depended on it," Miles growled.

<Um, now would be a good time.>

The nifty piece of hacker tech I'd slapped onto the bioscanner should have worked and let Cain slip in behind us.

"I wouldn't have betrayed you if you hadn't played me for a fool," Cain snarled as he entered the room, his gun trained on Miles.

3

Here Comes the Snag

Standoffs—always a tense situation, and putting myself in the middle of one wasn't a smart move.

Upsetting the crazed would-be emperor hadn't been the plan. We'd quickly figured out Miles High ran the show, since no one would budge on helping us unless Miles gave the say-so. So when all sane—or slightly less risky—avenues of getting off the station had been closed to us, I'd proposed seeing what Miles High was offering. Because for whatever reason, Miles had decided to take an interest in me. And only me.

The invitations had started a day after we landed on the station. They were addressed only to me—never to Cain and never with a plus one. They were all for Miles's nightly club show. The interest quickly turned into an obsession, based upon the number of invitations. The hitch was that I wasn't keen on going anywhere without Cain, who was less than thrilled about the idea as well.

So I'd gathered up the invites, arrived at the designated location, and stated Cain was my security. Denied. I figured the snub was against Cain and the fact he was still IGJ and of mixed-species heritage. It's maddening and sad how purist ideology propaganda runs deep, even all the way out on a junk heap of a station.

After the no-go with Cain as my security, the Shilo-Torp shadow had been next on Miles's creepy-stalker agenda. So, taking a page out of popular jute-store thrillers, Cain decided a little ruse was in order.

Hooking the rather dim-witted Shilo-Torp on our little love spats didn't take much —I use the term "love spat" loosely, mind you—although the longer we stayed at the station, the less we had to feign the whole "spat" part.

And don't forget that little stumble at the door. I certainly wasn't that clumsy. I had to do something to allow me to subtly stick the bioscanner with a ghoster, a nifty piece of tech that renders a security system inoperable for fifty-seven seconds—just under the one-minute mark, before redundant backup systems kick in. Enough time for a certain IGJ agent to follow.

Help desk aficionado, at your service. At least, I was before my Wepli bosses put a contract out on me. Anyway, upon pairing my useful knowledge of tech specs with Confore's need to stamp its tech with their logo, making it easy to identify, the whole system was a breeze to beat.

That should catch everyone up, right? Except for me—because Cain had obviously failed to mention a few key things.

"If you hurt her, you're dead," Cain snarled. He blinked, and his violet eyes were suddenly as black as the Chasm of Doom on Katrr.

"I feel I'm missing some information about the two

of you that I should know," I quipped, trying to lighten the tension and relax the hand with the sharp nails digging into my neck.

It didn't help.

"Get this piece of filth out of my club," Miles snapped the order as he twisted around me and shoved a weapon into my back.

Cain ducked the Shilo-Torp's armored fist. What the species lacked in speed, they more than made up for in nearly impossible-to-destroy plating. Natural keratin shells were enhanced with military-grade armor plates and shielding. Stamina was about the only thing someone like Cain had going for him. Moving a Shilo-Torp's massive bulk took a lot of energy, even with bioupgrades. If a Shilo-Torp's opponent could dodge and weave in a close-quarter attack long enough, the opponent would simply wear the Shilo-Torp out.

Unfortunately, considering my fellow audience member, I didn't think that was going to be an option. Miles would shoot Cain if push came to shove.

"I'll do it," I said. "I'll deliver your message."

"I might be reconsidering the offer," Miles grumbled.

"But you said I had connections. Even though you haven't clarified that bit, it sounds like you need me," I countered.

His breath was hot against my neck as he whispered in my ear, "Star Eaters."

Pluto's dilemma. "Who says I have connections with those crazy psychos?" I asked.

"My ears, darling. My little ears scurry everywhere."

I tried to shake the mental image of solitary ears

running around on cartoon legs. *Who's up for nightmares tonight?* "Let's say, for argument's sake—" I winced as the Shilo-Torp landed a heavy blow in the middle of Cain's back.

<*You've got to duck and weave.*> To be polite, I won't share Cain's sarcastic reply.

"But let's say I do have an in with the Star Eaters. What would you want with them?" I asked.

"That's none of your business. All I need is the message delivered. My ears tell me there's a small cluster of the fools on Lunar 5. They've refused my regular couriers, and something tells me those Star Eaters just might accept an invitation if I drop your name. Or they might eat you on the spot," Miles answered.

A lot of things were wrong with that. "First of all, ears don't have mouths. It's your lips or whatever talking to you. And second of all—" I popped my head back against his and rammed my heel right into his sweet spot.

I spun around, and the man's expression might have been amusing if not for the live-or-die situation. Right then, all I cared about was how to gain the upper hand.

I pushed back the sleeve of my jumpsuit and activated my Vulture DR-31, a significant upgrade from the Raptor-series weapon I had on the *Rapscallion.*

Vulture tech was black market, coded with a myriad of shielding protocols and nifty add-ons that ensured the weapon remained a high-demand product, and it was available in several stylish forms. I'd chosen Debutante's Best Pal, a sleek model designed to look like a knockoff replica of the armbands currently in fashion on Cloud 11. The bracelet had an ebony shell decorated with intricate scrollwork and rubies. Staying true to the whole knockoff bait and switch, my rubies were fake. I wasn't about to waste credits on the real deal, not when that version was still a fully functional weapon.

Within a heartbeat, the Vulture rearranged itself into a full-sleeve gun, the same base design as the Raptor with several added kicks, high-intensity disruptors and a scrambler. After I purchased my new accessory, I'd spent a few nights setting the Vulture to my specifications.

With my weapon trained on Miles, I confidently ordered, "Stop them."

Miles threw me a wink. He didn't think I was serious. I pressed the trigger and fired. A beautiful scorch mark appeared on the tile between his legs.

"There's no need for that." Miles frowned. "Rot, stand down."

"Rot?" I asked. "That's his name?"

The Shilo-Torp didn't answer but did at least follow his boss's instructions.

Thank Jupiter, because I'd been bluffing.

Cain frequently told me that defending myself and deliberately taking another's life were two different things. The IGJ had heaps of laws and case examples to back up Cain's arguments whenever I needed reminding that the events with Mrs. Gol and the two assassins fell into the defense category. While I understood and agreed with it all on an intellectual level, I couldn't shake the guilt that weighed on me. I was still responsible for those deaths.

And all those evenings spent watching true-crime dramas had taught me one thing. Becoming comfortable with death was easy. Not to wax too philosophical, but I often wondered if the reason was that when someone killed, a little piece of them was killed in the process. Or maybe the act snatched away some of the innocence everyone was born with, and deadening ourselves to those feelings became easier than living with them day in and day out.

If my father was researching a particularly nasty bit of history, he would always tell my brother and I that we shouldn't let our circumstances dictate what type of person we were, that we all had a choice in how we lived our lives.

I wondered what my father would say if I asked him how that applied to all the people he'd killed on the *Rapscallion*.

"So, the job?" Miles asked as Cain limped up beside me.

While I bluffed and deliberated the finer points on morality, I had no doubt Cain wouldn't. He would take the shot if need be.

"First, I would like to know what happened between you two," I asked. *<Seems like there are some details of this plan you could have told me.>*

<You weren't getting anywhere.>

<I was until I brought up your name. Could have at least given me a heads-up,> I countered.

Miles narrowed his eyes and looked back and forth between us. "Have you found your heart's blood?"

Cain growled and leaped forward. He grabbed a fistful of Miles's shirt and jabbed his gun under the man's chin. "Give us transport off your little heap of rubble."

Miles grinned, crimson-stained teeth bared for all to see. "Why would I help you?"

"Because I'm the one with a gun to your face, you miserable little piece of—"

"Enough." I was getting tired of their back-and-forth. "Get to the point. You need me to deliver a message, and we need transport to Lunar 5. Do we have a deal or not?"

I added Miles's little question about "heart's blood" to my growing list of information Cain needed to spill.

A fair amount of disgust showed on Miles's face as he considered everything.

"Must not be too pressing a message?" I asked, trying to speed things along.

His eyes snapped over to mine. "Oh, it is. I assure you." After another snarl between the two men, Miles went limp. "Fine. We have a deal. Just get off me."

Cain didn't move.

<Come on. We've got what we wanted,> I thought.

<Not until we're safely tucked away on Lunar 5, out of the reach of this… thing, then we've got what we wanted.>

Cue eye roll. Cain was still as insufferable as ever.

"I'm assuming that if I harm Ms. Orion in any way, you'll kill me?" Miles asked.

Cain nodded.

"And I'm also working under the assumption that if I kill this annoying piece of meat, you'll kill me too? Or at least do a fair amount of damage?" Miles asked me.

I might have paused a bit too long as Cain threw me a nasty look.

"Yup," I said.

"Surely, you can see we are at an agreement. Even though I find it distasteful to have to work"—Miles grimaced—"around him."

<*Come on,*> I whined. <*We need to get to Lunar 5 and start investigating what happened to Jorge. That's the priority, remember?*>

I didn't need Cain to respond mentally or vocally to feel his conflict. His tail snapping back and forth was enough.

"Fine," Cain spat and let Miles go.

Cain stepped back to stand shoulder to shoulder with me. "But if you do something I don't like… well, no hard feelings."

Miles hopped up and brushed himself off. "Sure. Whatever you say, pal."

"So, about this message," I said, feeling like a broken record.

"Dinner first, then we'll talk specifics."

Cain snarled and took a step in front of me. "No, we do this now. Get it over with."

"My longtime frenemy, the ship doesn't leave dock for another three hours. Plenty of time. Besides, what Rot has told me is the two of you have been eating a fair amount of swill. I presume you would like a decent meal before you go? I can't vouch for what you might find on Lunar 5."

The man had the audacity to shudder. Lunar 5 was a step up—heck, it was ten steps up from Epsilon's Station.

<*I am hungry.*>

"It's not my fault you didn't eat the zip," Cain mumbled.

I powered down the Vulture and decided to let Cain worry about defensive maneuvers. "Let's eat."

Miles clapped his hands, and I swear he jumped for joy. "Goodie!" he exclaimed then spun around and whistled. "Chef, dinner for three, please." He motioned at us. "Come, come. Up we go."

I glanced over at Cain, who shrugged. I recalled a saying, something from an Old Earth story about going down a rabbit hole. But in that case, up, up, up we went.

4

Deals and Meals

Miles led us to the highest balcony and gestured for us to take seats around the table there. As I sat, my gaze fell upon the tabletop. I looked over at Miles, aghast. "Tell me this didn't come from the Spires of Pola Tahh."

"I hoped you might recognize it. You have quite the travel history. Not to mention the adventures I'm sure come from being the daughter of the notorious Wats Hawking Orion," Miles replied gleefully. He turned his attention back to the tabletop. "Original piece. Taken from the Holy Triune's personal chambers. Over fifteen thousand years old. I spent a fortune to have it shipped here and inlaid." He held up a hand and looked serious for a split second. "Don't fret. I paid for the highest package possible. Gen fifty-one tech on smart-glass protection. Can't even tell, can you?"

I let out a long, low whistle. That kind of tech was reserved for the elite of the elite. But Miles was an ex-monarch. "What happened to the rest of it? If I remember right, this is a part of a larger scene. One of three, actually."

Miles nodded and reverently swept his hands across the image. "You remember correctly. The Three Heralds, one for each branch of the Tahh religion. But during the Cricade War, there were skirmishes around Pola Tahh. The capital city and its historical district took fire. I'm told there's another collector who tried to save parts of the other two scenes. But I've never gotten solid intel on who exactly that is. Sneaky rat."

"Look, see?" I grinned and glanced over at Cain.

He was still watching Miles but gave a nod. My enthusiasm dimmed, but I decided I wasn't going to let him get out of a lecture. That was a holdover from my father.

"This is a perfect example of the fifteenth cycle of art for the Tahhs. The long brushstrokes were painted during the thirteen cycle, and see here." I leaned over and pointed at several icons laced through the painting. "These are small pieces of mosaic. That's what makes the fifteenth cycle stand out. It was the fashion to recycle older pieces of art and add these intricate mosaics—never to fully disrupt the original intention behind the piece of art, only to enhance it."

<*It's quite a spectacular piece of work,*> Cain thought.

A part of me did relax at Cain's comment. For a brief moment, I could pretend we were engaged in normal conversation—no assassins, murdered IGJ agents, unwanted revelations about my father—just a group of friends learning and debating the finer points of another culture, something I hadn't done in years.

"Have you studied Cresta Lop Tahh? I have a few other pieces of her work. Some of the finest mosaics on the market," Miles said.

My brain ran with it and leaped at the chance to engage. "I have," I murmured, running my hands over the piece. "She's usually the first artist mentioned in reference to this cycle of art."

"Here," Miles said as he reached over and pressed down on the glass where one of my hands had come to rest. "Press and hold for three seconds over any part of the image."

I couldn't help but grin as I scanned the tabletop and chose one of the icons, a beautiful rendering of a capsa tree haloed by one of Pola Tahh's twin suns. An info box popped up, and I read through it with relish.

Capsa tree. A sacred plant on Pola Tahh. Religious texts and pre-third-cycle writings also include the capsa tree in a wide variety of well-known myths and folklore. The majority of these pre-third-cycle traditions state the capsa tree was a gift from The One, from which sprang The Two, who are most often represented as the twin suns, Po and La.

Despite academic debates regarding who or what The One represented or might have been, historic biological studies appear to confirm the capsa tree isn't a native species to Pola Tahh, and the idea of a genetically engineered tree has been raised. If the hypothesis of genetic engineering is to be considered, the question must be asked: Where did the technological knowledge come from for such a feat?

The original thirteenth-cycle artist chose to depict only Po illuminating a single capsa tree. Why the artist decided to go against standard beliefs that the twin suns should always be shown together is unknown and of particular interest to scholars who study this period of art.

During the fifteenth cycle, the well-documented artist Cresta Lop Tahh worked on this part of The Three Heralds for two years. Each individual mosaic tile was chipped and shaped by Cresta, ignoring the standard practice of purchasing the tiles from well-known tile makers, which often added another layer of prestige and value to this style of art.

"I didn't know that," I murmured as I ran my hand over the image. "Just an infinite number of creative energies on an infinite number of worlds, creating an infinite combination of art."

Miles nodded as he leaned forward and stared at the painting. "It's a pity so much of it will—"

Whatever he was going to impart, he didn't. Dinner arrived.

I eyed the sumptuous spread of food with a bit of trepidation. It wouldn't be the first time someone tried to trick me with food. I looked up at Miles, who smirked.

"Don't fret. The food from my kitchens are vetted," he said.

"Doesn't really mean anything to me anymore," I said.

"And if you find yourself with a touch of food poisoning, how does that help me?" he asked.

Logically, it didn't. I glanced over at Cain, who gave me a small nod of approval. *<He's many things, but he has a point. He needs you right now. The food should be safe.>*

<Here goes nothing, then.>

I'm not ashamed to admit that I requested seconds. I really tried to show restraint in that type of situation, eating with criminal masterminds, but I was hungry— not to mention the concern that it might be the last decent meal I would see for some time.

Cain stayed silent throughout the meal, one hand rested on his gun while the other speared minuscule portions. Miles engaged me in friendly banter, and my illusion of normalcy was allowed to continue.

Unfortunately though, the meal couldn't last forever.

Miles dabbed at his face with a napkin and waved a hand for the dishes to be cleared. He leaned back and, in classic bad-guy fashion, pressed his hands together and rested his chin on his forefingers.

"Blood type?" he asked.

I choked on my water. "Excuse me?"

"I'll need to know for the letter," Miles replied.

"You said it needed to be delivered the old-fashioned way. Paper and an envelope, right?"

Cain leaned forward with a frown, "No. Old-fashioned means encrypted files dispersed on smart-bots, nano sized and injected into your bloodstream. Small enough and benign enough not to trigger security alarms. If the courier would die, it doesn't matter. The message is still safely tucked away in their blood."

My days of watching true-crime dramas were letting me down. I'd never heard about that type of message-delivery system.

"And how is the message retrieved?" I hesitated to ask but kind of needed to know since I'd agreed to be the courier and all.

"A simple procedure," Cain continued to explain. "The recipient has the coding information, and to not get lost in the jargon, picture the setup like a magnet. The intended recipient places this magnet on, say, your arm, and the smart-bots are attracted to it, and so your blood is drawn. The procedure typically takes two or three blood draws all in all."

<No harm to the courier,> he added for my benefit.

"Give the man a fuel cell," Miles quipped with a halfhearted clap. He straightened in his chair and snapped his fingers. From the shadows stepped not one but three Shilo-Torps.

I shouldn't have gotten lost in the facade of normalcy.

The giant Shilo-Torps clamped down on our shoulders and easily kept us seated. Cain shifted his grip on his gun. I knew what he wanted to do, and while I might've been Miles's current tool of interest, a man of resources would undoubtedly be able to find another.

<If you fire, we're as good as dead,> I warned Cain.

<It would be satisfying.> Cain let the thought slip out to me.

<Be that as it may, don't.>

Before Cain could make a decision, the third Shilo-Torp reached forward and snatched Cain's gun.

The abrupt shift from polite conversation to an outright reminder of who we were dealing with had me tasting a little of that glorious supper once more. We were adrift and at the mercy of a self-made madman. We might've been sitting in one of the largest spaces on the station, but I felt the walls closing in as the Shilo-Torp held me in place. My heart was racing, along with my thoughts.

Cain tried to be reassuring. <*We'll figure a way out.*>

His words didn't help as Miles stood and pulled out some type of syringe. <*Well, at least if I'm going to be poisoned again, I know what's coming.*>

The criminally insane man held up the syringe and studied its design as he talked. "These instruments haven't changed much from their first inception on Old Earth. Centuries-old technology. Except this has a slight modification developed by my great-grandfather. With the increasing number of species one might engage a little subterfuge with, he developed an adaptable needle, capable of puncturing even the toughest hide or delicately piercing human skin without leaving a mark. Eliminates the need for keeping a wide variety of needles on hand. Certainly a breeze to travel with."

"Gloat much?" I asked.

"Of course." Miles grinned extra wide. "Especially when I have a captive audience." His grin fell when neither one of us laughed. "Tough sell."

"Old joke," Cain growled.

"Yes, well…" Miles sniffed. "You'll find most of the old-school black market tech was developed by my ancestors and other ruling elite throughout the settled worlds. Not a big revelation, I know." His gaze found mine as he grinned afresh. "But makes sense, doesn't it? Governments always have secrets to trade back and forth." He turned his waste-eating grin on Cain. "Isn't that right?"

I knew what was coming and tried to struggle, to

find a weakness I could exploit in the all-too-powerful grip of the Shilo-Torp. But my captor was earning its five-star rating as muscle for hire.

Miles walked around the table like an old-school villain, probably hearing some sort of suspenseful music in his head. As he walked, the Shilo-Torps masterfully maintained their grip on the two of us while simultaneously sliding our chairs apart. Miles stopped and stood between us.

"It won't hurt a bit," Miles commented dryly. He leaned forward and jammed the needle into my forearm.

I braced for the pain, figuring when someone said, "It won't hurt a bit," they were lying in an effort to try to make me feel better. But I really felt no pain and didn't even see a mark.

Pity. That would have given me something to complain about, to milk the situation for all it was worth. I mean, for crying out loud, there I was, once again the object of people's ill-begotten attention. History was finding a way to repeat itself.

I looked up at Miles and batted my eyelashes. "Do I get a sucker?"

Miles chuckled and shook his head. "Nope. Something far better."

With a flourish, he pulled out a second syringe, turned, and plunged it into the side of Cain's neck.

Cain snarled and bared his teeth. "You'll pay for this."

"Add it to the list," Miles retorted. "You're still keeping a list, aren't you? I've got mine."

"What did you just do?" I asked as my panic increased.

Miles's grin turned horrific as he tossed the syringe and held out a hand, and the Shilo-Torp handed him the gun he'd taken from Cain. Miles turned the weapon back and forth, disengaged the safety, and pointed the muzzle at Cain's head.

5

Insurance Policies

"If you kill him, I won't deliver your message." I blurted the words without thinking. "Don't get me wrong, Cain is as annoying as the whole debate over Pluto being a planet or not, but right now, he's my partner."

I had expected some glib telepathic remark from Cain, but I sensed only his presence tickling the base of my skull. He remained silent as he turned to look at me. His coal-black irises lightened to amber, and I kid you not, the man blushed then let his gaze brush past me to stare out into the club.

Miles rolled his eyes. "Annoying doesn't even begin to describe it, darling." He slid the muzzle down and pressed it into Cain's neck, forcing him to lift his chin.

"Don't worry. I'm not about to coat either of us with his brains. My cleaning bill is high enough this month as it is. This is merely a visual aid"—Miles turned to stare at me—"in case you don't fully understand the rules. But you're a smart cookie. I'm sure you'll figure it out."

Please don't say it... Please don't...

"Because if you don't deliver the message, your *partner* dies."

He said it.

Cain decided to speak. "Another nifty invention of your family?" His Shilo-Torp captor shifted their hand to press down on the other side of Cain's throat.

"My own, thank you," Miles said. "Experience is a cruel mistress. I learned the hard way—couriers need an incentive to ensure they follow their assignments. So, I designed companion bots. Each nanobot is a twin to the smart-bots coursing through your"—he gave me a wink—"lovely blood. Both sets of bots monitor the other with a unique countdown system I had the distinct pleasure of programming."

"Countdown?" I asked.

"A one-week nonrefundable time limit."

He grinned and leaned into the pressure he was putting on Cain with the gun. "But if the message is delivered and retrieved on time, I'll personally guarantee the—let's call it the all-clear—message will be sent, and Cain's nanobots will deactivate."

"Deactivate but not be destroyed?" I asked.

"Clever little monkey," Miles murmured. "I'll send you the instructions on how to flush my little helpers out of his system as well."

I would believe that when I saw it.

"So if I miss the deadline to deliver the message, his nanobots deliver a nasty little surprise," I said.

Miles nodded. "If not extracted within the specified time"—with his free hand, he gestured—"they go boom."

"Boom, great, got it." What a wonderful picture—lots of tiny little bombs all floating around inside Cain.

<He loves games. We play by the rules, and we'll win,> Cain thought.

Cain was trying to comfort me, but I couldn't help myself. *<Speaking from experience?>*

"Are we free to go?" Cain asked Miles instead of responding to me. "We're on the clock."

Miles squinted at him then let out a long sigh. "Why not. Rot, escort them to their rooms. Let them pack then take them to the docking rings."

"I'm not sure that counts as letting us go," I added with my own long sigh of relief as the Shilo-Torps released us.

"Your charming IGJ agent can be a slippery eel at times." Miles shrugged. "Consider this an insurance policy."

"What, another one? You don't think impending death is good enough?" I fumed as I stood and glanced down at the tabletop. Works of art weren't sentient—except for Neetho creations, of course—but I felt a pang of pity for the Pola Tahh artwork. It had been created out of reverence for something far greater than its artists, only to end up serving as eye candy for a lunatic.

Miles caught my wistful look. "I can show you the rest of the collection. There is time—"

But Cain grabbed my arm and, with a low growl, shoved me in the direction of the stairs.

<Maybe I want to see it.>

<And maybe you don't.>

Letting Cain lead me, I glanced back to note that

Miles had stayed at the table and was staring off into the distance with a forlorn expression.

As much as I didn't want to, I couldn't help but wonder what his story was. He would've had everything on Old Earth. The criminal life held a certain type of romantic appeal, but I wondered why he'd left the monarchy. They held the power to change the course of history on a mere whim. Which they did, too many times and often not for the better. So I couldn't help but wonder why Miles had given up that kind of power to rule over a measly dump of a station.

"How do you know Miles?" I asked Cain without thinking.

I was pretty sure Cain wasn't going to answer as we followed Rot out of Miles's den of iniquity. But as we stepped out into the main terminal hub, Cain stopped and turned to stare at me.

"Do you really want to know?"

His question took me by surprise, but not as much as his look of sincerity. His violet eyes watched me, his lips pressed together into a thin line.

Cain was an attractive man, who—I'm not ashamed to admit—featured in the majority of my dreams since we'd met. But attraction alone does not a good companion make. Too many true-crime dramas started off with attraction only to crumble into a web of lies and deception.

I'd experienced glimpses of the man hidden beneath the gruff exterior of an IGJ agent, moments when he offered me support with no request for something in return. I appreciated those offerings just as I appreciated his help in getting to the bottom of why Confore wanted me dead and how they believed I was tangled up with the IGJ's investigation.

I understood Cain's need to solve the case, to gain the clout he needed to help his sister. But Cain could have theoretically done all that without my help.

And now, we had this little side gig of playing messenger, complete with an impending-doom scenario that ran the highly probable chance of delaying Cain's goals—permanently.

As I stared at Cain, a revelation hit me like an unexpected grav-dump. He was voluntarily offering a glimpse into who he really was—not surface information or his understandable need to help his sister. If I said yes, Cain would share a part of his life that defined him, something undoubtedly deeply personal and, I suspected, known by few.

"No." The word came out broken, and I cleared my head. "No, let's stay focused. We've got a time crunch now."

So call me a coward.

I wasn't ready for that level of sharing. I knew Cain had seen and heard a lot on the *Rapscallion*, but that hadn't been us sitting down and having a heart-to-heart. We'd been pieces on a chessboard, moved around according to Mrs. Gol's preferences.

At the moment, we were using each other. Cain needed to help his sister, and I needed to get Confore off my back in order to figure out the truth about my father so that no one could use it against me again.

I moved past Cain, not wanting to see his reaction.

I thought of those info-adverts that flashed images of Old Earth bio-inspired pets left abandoned and forgotten—guaranteed instatears.

So instead, we moved through the terminal in silence with Rot trailing behind. I should've been more concerned over the whole situation than I felt. But I wasn't. Perhaps having played one death game already had numbed me to the next.

Thank Jupiter the terminal wasn't overflowing with business, which meant we only had to wait a few seconds for a lift.

It was a tight squeeze, with Rot's bulk added to the mix. Smashed up against the Shilo-Torp in a space featuring minimal air recycling, I realized how Rot had earned his name. I had no doubt that if I'd been able to access a mirror, it would have reflected my newly minted greenish skin tone.

Epsilon's Station had originally been built by humans for humans, back in the golden age of space exploration when relationships with other species were in their infancy. The station was one of the oldest still in use, which said a lot.

Stations and ships—anything, really—just weren't built like they used to be. Perhaps as the worlds opened up and resources became plentiful, companies produced products guaranteed to need repairs or upgrades at regular intervals. But despite the old-school craftsmanship, the station limped along due to the ingenuity of its maintenance crews.

We exited the lift, and Rot had to retract his head nearly all the way into his shell in order to keep from banging it against the corridor's supports. He might've been there to enforce his boss's orders, but I did feel sorry for the guy.

"Rot, why don't you wait here? The room isn't any bigger. We'll get our gear and be back in a flash," I suggested.

The Shilo-Torp leaned forward to poke his head out just enough for his beak to open and close a few times in uncertainty. A low hiss escaped before his AI Voca-box kicked in. "I have orders to ensure the *frothli* doesn't try to escape."

The implied threat would've held a lot more weight if not for that silly AI voice. I opened my mouth to make that suggestion when Cain stepped up next to Rot. He stretched until he was standing on tiptoe and reached out to touch the top of Rot's shell. An unexpected move, but then again, Cain was IGJ. They were certainly trained in understanding a wide variety of biologies and how to calm down potential aggressors. Shilo-Torps showed trust and affection by rubbing their heads against the top of another's shell. In that case, it was the best imitation Cain could do.

"I'll behave."

After another low hiss and a few more beak-clacking gestures, Rot said, "Ten minutes. Then I follow."

"Agreed."

6

The Highest Bid Always Wins

We didn't have much gear to pack. Each of us had a couple of spare sets of clothes and the weapons we'd purchased upon arrival at the station. So we were in and out before Rot's countdown got close to requiring any kind of body handling.

<Are you sure there are no side effects to this whole human-body-messenger thing?> My arm was beginning to itch where I'd been injected. *<Where's a master when you need one?>* I joked.

Cain glanced down at my arm at a small red ring forming. "You'll be fine."

Great. Open mouth and insert boot. <I was only trying to lighten the mood. Since there's impending doom on the horizon and all.>

Cain opened his mouth then snapped it shut. *<Just stay focused. Miles is always up to no good.>*

"I think I got that when he injected you with the death bots," I mumbled.

We got back onto the lift, Cain on one side of Rot, while I was squeezed in on the opposite side for the ride back down to the main terminal. Without any time for a fond farewell speech to the station or a nostalgic moment to ponder life's greatest questions, Rot ushered us toward the docking rings.

The main terminal was connected to the docking rings via another terminal. The space operated on stim-pills, always green-lit for rush hour traffic. Travelers debated the merits of overnighting on the station while waiting for connections or finding an alternative route. Neethos and others hawked vouchers, fresh jumpsuits, and a myriad of goods they worked hard to convince shoppers were necessary—not to mention the low-atmosphere prices and lifetime credit-back guarantees. One would think the scam traps would be standard traveler-beware zones, but that wasn't so. I shook my head at the steady stream of eager customers.

"Where to?" I asked Rot.

"Docking Ring Five, the *Whimsy.*"

"Charter or cargo?" Cain inquired.

"Cargo."

"Does it matter?" I asked.

Cain shrugged and continued to follow Rot. I mentally sent him a few choice replies, to which his only response was a slight hitch in his shoulders. *Infuriating man.*

Rot's bulk helped clear the way through the docking terminal, and we took another lift to the specified docking ring. Our ring didn't have a crowd, thank Jupiter. In fact, the whole dimly lit space looked abandoned, lacking workers buzzing about—not to mention the Under Construction and Repairs holos greeting us.

"You sure this is the right place?" I asked as I moved my opposite hand to hover over the Vulture.

"Oh, he's sure."

The voice preceded a volley of weapon fire that lit up the space like the annual celebration of Liberation Nights. An unexpected shove sent me spinning off to the right, and as I scrambled for cover behind a stack of containers, I activated the Vulture.

With a few deep breaths to calm my nerves, I searched for Cain.

<*Where are you?*> I thought.

<*Over here, to your left.*>

All annoyance was forgotten. Relief flooded through me as I searched the shadows cast by a few forgotten panels of hull. Cain was crouched down behind them.

<*You'd better still be alive.*>

<*I am, but I'm afraid our friend won't be for long.*>

Rot's body had fallen where we were standing seconds before. Smoke wafted up from the giant Shilo-Torp, and I was close enough to hear the hiss as some type of acrid substance ate its way through his armor. Everything had a weakness, even a Shilo-Torp.

The Shilo-Torp's presence had grown on me, and watching him die did hurt. We were never pals or anything, but the big guy had been shadowing us for several days. *Is a recon buddy a thing?* Besides, I knew whose hand had shoved me. Yes, Rot was acting on orders or perhaps a sense of loyalty to his boss, but his shove had pushed me to safety.

But I wasn't a poison-control expert, and even if I had a clue as to what might work as a counteragent, I doubted I could find anything nearby.

<Whoever did this knew what they were doing. They were prepared. There's nothing we can do for Rot now,> Cain sent.

Cain was trying to get me to focus on the immediate threat, but a shiver ran through me at what appeared to be such a callous response.

"We've no interest in killing you," a female called out. "Or your pet."

Pet? Given the fact Rot was dying, I knew whom they were referring to.

"He's not my pet!" I shouted.

<Leave it.>

<No.>

"Sure looks like he would be nice to cuddle with," someone else snickered. "Something a little outside-of-the-box to experiment with?"

"Not much else they're good for, these muddled breeds," a third person chimed in.

"You wouldn't happen to know Mrs. Fairhaven Gol, would you?" I asked.

"What?" the female asked.

"Nothing. Just figured purist scum ran in the same circles."

I realized I probably shouldn't have said that as someone let off a fresh round of weapon fire.

"Hold fire," the female snapped. "They want them alive."

I learned two things. First, at least three people were shooting at us, and the female was in charge. Second, they were working on behalf of someone else. *The Tretoono Club perhaps?* That would make sense—retribution for what had happened on the *Starshine.*

"Little hard to believe with that warm greeting you gave us," I stated. "Besides, we're dead anyway if we can't complete our job."

<We're dead?> Cain inquired.

<Close enough.>

"Miles playing at one of his games again, is he?" one of the males asked. "No matter. They'll see to it you live. At least for as long as you have value to them, anyway."

"Shut it," the female snapped.

"If you've got any cheat sheets, maybe we can work something out," I suggested, thinking it was worth a shot.

"Oh, we want to make a deal, just not with you. Don't misunderstand, but we got ourselves a one-time offer we couldn't refuse," the female said.

"You're simply the commodity, see?" one of the male voices added.

Honor amongst thieves, eh?

"Perhaps we can negotiate our own terms," Cain interrupted.

The male laughed and was joined by the other, who then said, "I highly doubt either one of you can afford our terms."

"Try me," Cain growled. The shadow I assumed was him moved.

"Oh, we know exactly who you are, and trust us, you can't afford it."

<I'll move, then you move to this position.>

<Really? Not ordering me to stay put? Stay out of the way?>

Irritation permeated the telepathic link. *<I would. But we both know you won't listen.>* After a pause, he sent, *<Count down from three then give me cover fire. Once I'm in place, I'll draw their attention. Move fast. Stay low. Then stay put.>*

<Can't help yourself, can you?> I snickered.

He did have a point. The metal sheeting was cover superior to my current wall of container boxes. I squinted off into the murky darkness and counted. *Three… two… one.*

I leaned around the edge of the containers and fired. A container to my left exploded in an array of fragments, and I curled up into a ball, trying to protect my head from the worst of the shrapnel.

"Don't kill her." The frantic command made me smirk as I realized being a high-value target did have its perks at times. "Only flesh wounds. Enough to slow them down."

Okay, maybe I was wrong about the perks. I uncurled, took aim, and fired off a few more shots.

<Get ready.>

"Behind you, Captain," one of the male voices barked.

The cadence of the weapon's fire changed from the powerful booms of our adversary's weapons to rapid-fire, whiplike cracks.

Cain's gun. It was a Krisper F-2, standard issue for IGJ agents, built from the specs of Old Earth weaponry before humans left their ball of dirt but upgraded for combat in the precarious spaces of ships and stations. Smart bullets were all the rage not too soon after humans began to colonize the moon, and they're the only human-based tech crammed full of more sensors than a Glipglow's nail. Each bullet carried an array of heat and biosensors, programmed with target locks and tracking capabilities, designed to seek flesh-and-bone targets without puncturing a hole in an outer hull wall.

Black market peddlers did offer deflecting gear and scramblers, but I'd learned from my time working in the tech business that no matter what the black market churned out, the IGJ stayed a step ahead of them.

As Cain fired, I ran from behind the containers and past Rot, then I dove behind the panel pieces. I heard a few unnecessary words and a couple of groans from our assailants.

<Good work,> I thought.

Unfortunately, another round of weapon fire started, and when Cain didn't respond, my gut fluttered nervously. My brain might've been dancing around my feelings for the IGJ man, but my annoying heart wasn't.

When he remained silent, I went with the option of doing something foolish.

"I'll come out. I surrender. Just don't kill Cain," I called out.

I deactivated the Vulture, slipped it off, and threw it over the containers. "See? I'm unarmed." Knowing it was a stupid move but betting on my status as a precious commodity, I stood with my hands in the air and moved out from behind the panels.

"Three steps forward then stand still," the female snapped.

Those were directions I could follow.

A red light lit up the shadows in front of me, and a scanner sprang to life. Its focused light ran over me.

"She's clean," one of the males commented.

"Duh. I said I was unarmed," I muttered.

The light blinked twice and shut down, and out from the shadows stepped three humans. Cautiously, they moved forward with the two men flanking the woman while continually checking the perimeter.

"Where's Cain?" I demanded.

The woman pursed her lips and stared at me. Her auburn hair was streaked with gray, and her eyes and mouth were framed by wrinkles. If I was forced to guess, I would say she was a decade or two older than myself.

Her flight suit was dated and boasted an impressive number of patches, while her two goons were decked out in flashy jumpsuits constructed from olepath cloth, manufactured solely by the Glipglows. All the rage, the jumpsuits were light, breathable, and programmed with nanotech so that the suit could easily morph into a functional space suit. It wasn't a long-term solution, but in a pinch, the suit provided protection for up to twelve hours.

The woman's face darkened, and she took a threatening step forward. "He's fine."

Blood was dripping down the face of the man standing to the woman's left, and I was ready to give Cain another attaboy when a bright light pierced the gloom. Squeezing my eyes shut, I threw up an arm to shield myself from the worst of it and felt the abrupt sensation of something on fire tearing across my skin.

With a yelp, I instinctively crouched and scuttled

off for cover, only to run into a solid wall of armor. After a rather ungraceful tumble backward, I looked up. Another Shilo-Torp had its head fully extended, beak open and hissing. Thankfully, it wasn't focused on me but on what stood behind me.

"Captain Markea. Oh dear. Oh dear... oh dear, oh dear."

My head snapped to the side, and I'll admit I sagged in relief. *Miles.*

The man sauntered forward, flashing his cane with each step. "Did you think you could steal from me?"

"I found a better deal is all. You know how it goes."

I tipped my head back to stare at the upside-down image of the woman. She hadn't budged. In fact, she looked quite relaxed. *Not good.* I scrambled to my feet and moved to keep the Shilo-Torp and two other companions in front of me. I wondered how many Miles kept on retainer.

"Oh, sweetie, I'd thought we'd moved beyond these things," Miles shook his head. "I pay far more than the Tretoono Club ever will."

"While your competitors are offering a hefty sum for these two, there is another bid that far outstrips yours or the Club's. Enough to cover hauling fees and necessary bribes and leave us all with a nice chunk of credits left over," Captain Markea replied. "Not to mention the one thing you can't give us."

"Is that so?" Miles shook his head then glanced down at his hand holding the cane. His index finger tapped the side once, twice, then a third time.

"I would have been willing to negotiate if you hadn't

gone and killed one of my employees. I pay fair wages with health policies, retirement plans, and life insurance. And I honor those agreements, which means you've cost me a fair amount of expenditures this quarter, which I'd hoped to avoid. Accountants, they're creatures of details."

"Walk away, and you can have a share of the profit," the woman said and crossed her arms.

She had guts—I had to give her that.

Miles nodded again. "Gracious of you."

He twirled his cane then pointed it at the captain and her men. Miles looked back at me and winked. "But it seems I have an agreement I need to keep instead."

Without further warning, bolts of electricity shot out from the tip of his cane. Streaks of searing-hot lines of white-and-blue light danced across the captain and her two men. Their horrifying screams filled the air as their skin bubbled and popped, and steam wafted off their bodies as they collapsed to the ground.

I quickly turned away as my stomach rolled. The nauseating acrid stench of burnt flesh greeted me with each sharp inhalation.

"My apologies. I forgot which setting I had it on." Miles sniffed and turned toward his henchmen. "Topper, get rid of the mess. Licks, see to the IGJ man." He pulled out an old-fashioned handkerchief and held it up to his nose. "Oh, and do something about the smell."

I stood there and gaped, having no words.

"Just something I've whipped up. An experiment, really."

"Something you whipped up?" I asked. "You

electrocuted three people. Fried them like…" I stopped. I didn't know what it was like, and I didn't want to try to conjure up an analogy.

"So?" Miles gave me a puzzled look.

Cain had said Miles enjoyed his games, but that wasn't some family game night. It was life or death with a man who didn't play by the rules.

Covering my mouth and nose to try to stop the worst of the stench, I shoved my way past Miles and his victims. Or at least, I tried to.

He flipped his cane and used the handle to reach out and hook my arm. "Not so fast."

"Let me go," I snapped and tried to shake him off.

Miles waltzed over and, in one smooth move, grabbed my hand while slipping the cane under his arm. "This won't do. If you leak, you leak my message." He twisted my arm back and forth in order to exam the burn. "Lucky."

I didn't know if I would have chosen that word to describe my current status.

He let go of me, turned, and cooed, "Come out, come out wherever you are."

Deciding the man had truly lost it, I took a few steps back, and when he didn't try to stop me, I darted off to find Cain. That wasn't hard—all I had to do was find the hulking mass of a Shilo-Torp, and presto, there they were.

A few meters away from the outer hull wall, the Shilo-Torp was letting Cain hold onto its arm to pull himself up to his feet. I skidded to a stop and started to reach out for Cain but stopped myself in time. My arms dropped to my sides, and I visually examined him for any injuries. *Keep it under control.*

A peculiar look settled on his face before he gave himself a shake and muttered, "I'm fine. The shielding held. But I'm going to need to recharge it soon."

"Good. Fine," I replied.

<Are you all right?> Cain asked.

I shivered and nodded. "Peachy. Always a thrill to watch people get electrocuted."

Cain's expression changed from wounded curiosity to rage. Those lovely violet irises disappeared into a sparkling emerald flecked with black. I didn't need any telepathic link to read the situation.

For a moment, I allowed my heart to revel in his fury for my sake—just a teeny, tiny moment. All right, maybe it was a little longer than that. Cain got several steps away from me before my brain kicked in. I spun around and raced after him.

"Don't. It's not worth it. You're only going to provoke him." And I meant every word.

Both men had made it abundantly clear they didn't like each other. Miles had just demonstrated how little he valued others' lives, and I couldn't prevent the image of Cain's body suddenly lying next to the others from popping up.

I had no control over my end of our link.

Cain stopped and turned. That time, I ignored my brain and followed my heart. I melted into his arms and buried my face against his shoulder.

Popular media has always had a way of desensitizing its viewers to violence. One look at jute-store novels and holomovie rankings will show a lot of titles to make one shiver. I always enjoyed a good adventure story jam-packed with action. But knowing something isn't real and actually witnessing it are two very different things.

<*The shock will wear off in time. The memory will dim.*>

I appreciated the truth, as well as the fact that he didn't give me sugarcoated platitudes, telling me I would be all right. No one should ever be all right after witnessing what I had.

Cain gently pushed me away and stared at me with liquid amber eyes. <*But right now, we need to move forward.*>

He was right. A time and place would come later, to work through my feelings, and that wasn't going to be the last incident to haunt my dreams for the foreseeable future.

"A touching moment between heart's blood," Miles quipped as he strode over.

"That's the second time you've mentioned that—" I started.

But Cain stepped forward. "What now?"

Miles looked around and, after a pointed sigh, said, "It would appear you've attracted more attention than I bargained for. And I don't like sharing." He turned a dazzling smile on both of us. "Turns out I will need to keep a closer eye on the two of you. Looks like I'm going with you. Keep up, now. We've got a schedule to keep."

7

Denied

The rest of the *Whimsy*'s crew didn't put up a fight. In fact, I would wager they'd been through that type of rapid turnover in command a few times before. No one questioned Miles as he took charge, and they continued to prep the ship without missing a beat. Roughly an hour after entering the docking ring to board the cargo vessel, we got the all clear to leave.

Cargo ships came in all sorts of shapes and sizes. Corporation-owned cargo vessels stripped out as much luxury as possible to cram every inch of the ship with assets. Crews were regulated to minuscule quarters, and on top of that, those cramped hab-units were shared with fellow crew members who worked opposite shifts. Midsize operations, typically run by generational family crews, found a healthy balance between optimal cargo space and crew space. Thankfully, the *Whimsy* appeared to have been originally built for a family operation before Miles commandeered the ship for his business ventures.

The trip from Epsilon's Station to Lunar 5 would take four days instead of the typical two weeks, thanks to Miles's investment in the ship's engine. Providing nothing interrupted us, we would be left with three days to deliver the message and hope Miles honored his end of the arrangement with the deactivation codes to Cain's nanobots.

The first thing Miles did once we got underway was to invite us on a tour as though we were all long-time buddies getting ready to snuggle down on vacation together. Declining the crazy man's offer definitely wasn't an option.

Miles droned on, at considerable length, about the great expenses he'd undertaken to ensure his fleet of ships were installed with the latest overdrive engines, not my area of expertise. Confore didn't build engines, but several such human companies existed, and most other species had at least a handful of companies that did as well. The market was crowded with engine tech, all clamoring to be the latest and greatest.

"Take a few moments to freshen up, then I insist the two of you join me for some refreshments." Miles bowed to us as he issued yet another mandatory invitation. "One of the crew will show you to your quarters."

Another polite way of telling us we aren't really guests. Who would've thought?

A sullen man who stepped out from behind Miles looked us up and down and said with a grunt, "Come on, then."

We climbed the stairs up to the deck with the crew quarters. The middle-aged man stopped at one of the doors and reached out to press a palm against its bioscanner. The back of his hand was covered in scars, with the edges of a few more under the cuff of his jumpsuit's sleeve. Maintaining any kind of ship was labor-intensive work and often deadly.

When the door opened, the man jerked his head to the side, clearly wanting us to get a move on so that he could be rid of us.

Cain moved first, gallantly taking the lead while I stepped up to the bioscanner. My gaze shot down to the lower right-hand corner, which displayed that pesky little Confore logo. At least I had a good idea of how the scanner worked. I honestly didn't think anything of it as I reached out to recode the scanner to my biometrics, but the crewman grabbed my wrist and twisted it away.

"Stays as is," he snapped. "This ain't no tour ship."

"Figures," I muttered, half tempted to put up a fight just out of spite.

But that ultimately wouldn't get me anywhere. He let go, and I stepped into the modestly sized room, glancing back at the interior wall, opposite where the bioscanner was situated on the outside.

Once the door closed, I decided to try to reconfigure the scanner behind the scenes. The wall's thickness was up to regulations, deep enough to accommodate standard food dispensers, Dash an' Wash stations, and a handful of other necessary tech on board a ship.

The majority of ship engineers and design companies maintained standard inward wall dimensions for two reasons. The size was optimal for cost-versus-safety ratios and had been in use for at least a century, which meant tech companies built their appliances to those specifications so that equipment could be easily replaced. And because tech was made to fit those standard wall dimensions, technicians had access to a unit from either side—perfect for red-light situations when parts of a ship might be locked down due to biohazards or hull breaches. I slid my hands around the edges of the bioscanner's back panel, found the trigger release, and popped the sucker off. I glanced over my shoulder, and Cain was doing whatever he thought was best, which was apparently scanning the room for bugs—tech bugs. At least I hoped that was the only type of bug he was concerned about.

"We're in luck," I commented. "Looks like the crew hasn't stripped the secondary parts for credits quite yet."

Older models of Confore tech came with built-in backup gear. In that case, a second bioscanner panel was available for when the first one went on the fritz. Frankly, I was impressed the original scanner hadn't already given out. Several years before, Confore had nixed the secondary backups in favor of forcing customers to upgrade to a newer, better, and much more expensive model. Replacement parts could be sourced, but they would cost an arm and a leg. Most customers bought into the membership rewards program Confore offered—without reading the fine print—with a minimal monthly fee for a measly percentage off any upgrade. Service fees, diagnostic fees, and a host of other stipulations ensured Confore still made a mint off their tech.

"Give me your hand." When the appendage didn't appear, I turned and frowned. "I won't bite."

"No, but the ship's records might."

"What?" I asked, a little put out by his lack of

compliments on my skills. "Do you want them to have the only access to our quarters?"

Cain sighed. "We add our biometrics into the scanner, and they're logged into the ship's central computer. That data is then stored for up to three years."

"And your point is?"

His tail whipped back and forth. "The point is anyone who could hack into the system can find us."

Oh. Well, fudge nuggets. I hadn't thought about that. "Well, excuse me for being out of practice with being on the run."

"It's standard IGJ training—"

"Don't care," I snapped as I popped everything back in place. "I'll just bow to your wisdom, oh great one."

Cain had a valid point, but for some reason, I didn't want to let him know that. Perhaps I'd been on my own for far too long. Or perhaps everything was beginning to spiral out of control again, and the only control I felt I had was by using what I knew. And he was, quite figuratively, stomping all over it.

"When we join Miles," Cain said, ignoring my little temper tantrum, "just keep quiet."

"Why?" I leaned back against the wall and stared at him.

"Because he knows how to get to you," Cain growled.

"Get to me? What's that supposed to mean?"

Too bad Rot was no longer with us. Cain and I were gearing up for a doozy of an argument.

"The art, that blasted tabletop. You drooled all over that thing. Not to mention how he suspects we're—" Cain stopped himself and turned away.

"What? What does he suspect?" I feared the answer, but I needed to hear him say it.

"Nothing," he snapped. "Just don't say anything. Let me do the talking."

"Oh, is that so, heart's blood?"

Cain whipped back around, and I swear the man cycled through all his known eye colors until they settled on a deep, dark emerald.

"Don't ever joke about that," Cain whispered. His shoulders were pulled back, muscles taut, hands balled into fists that dug into the sides of his thighs. *<Never.>*

For the first time since he'd rudely intruded on my thoughts, I felt the connection dim until it was nearly impossible to detect. I blinked at the abrupt absence, not realizing how easily I'd gotten comfortable with its presence. I knew I had my moments on the *Rapscallion* when I'd gone too far, but this was on an entirely new level.

We stood there in dreadful silence until the door opened and a young woman gave us a tight smile. "I've been asked to take you to the captain's quarters."

Cain moved past me without a word, and I slunk out of the room after them. I was worried. I knew Cain had multiple buttons that I enjoyed pushing, but I wondered if I'd finally gone too far. A question that sparked another uncomfortable question began to gnaw at me. *If we survive this game, will Cain leave me? And do I want him to or not?*

8

Open Mouth and Insert Foot

We were escorted to the captain's quarters, a room double the size of the one we'd been given. Miles was standing in the center next to a large oval table and, with arms wide open, gave us a huge grin as we entered.

"At last." He waved his hands at the woman. "Shoo. Go on, now. Shoo."

The table was cluttered with mismatched sets of dishes, all full to the brim with what promised to be mouthwatering food. The rich aromas made my stomach churn in a less-than-desirable fashion. *Does Miles retain a full set of kitchen staff wherever he goes?*

Cain took a seat at the table while I headed over to the corner and sat down on a plush couch bolted to the floor. I could feel Miles looking back and forth at the two of us, but I turned my head to stare out the modest window and did my best to ignore both of them.

"Lovers' spat?" Miles quipped.

"Run down Lunar 5." Cain didn't speak it as a question but a demand.

Out of the corner of my eye, while studiously trying

not to care, I saw Miles move. It took a lot of strength not to turn and acknowledge that I wanted to be a part of the conversation.

The honest truth was that I was weighing the pros and cons of sticking around with Cain. I've discussed my reasons for being a loner—my last name, my father's notorious reputation—and truth be told, life would've been far simpler on my own, with no one to worry about, to watch out for emotionally, or to demand anything from me.

That was one of the reasons I've continued to shoot down offers to turn my life into a series of jute-story novels. I have no doubt I would make a killing off them. People would eat up the tales of how I planet hopped as a kid, each new destination full of adventure. My childhood was the life many people dreamed about experiencing.

But the reality was a lot more complicated. My father's work meant months or years of isolation. We lived in remote locations with only a handful of coworkers or, at best, limited contact with other governmental or contracted organizations my father coordinated. The majority of those individuals were just as engrossed in the work as my father had been, and in that type of lifestyle, dragging your kids along with you wasn't common practice.

My brother and I learned the hard way how to live that kind of life. And after being abandoned by my brother and, in effect, my father, I figured I was better off on my own—no lasting connections, no entanglements to come back and bite me in the rear.

So, the twenty-four-hour question was "Why had I opened up to Cain? What made him so special? Was it the telepathic link?"

I could buy a Partner Assisted Telepath for cheap on almost any corner. PATs were a dime a dozen, touted as the ultimate tool to combat loneliness, isolation, and depression. In less than two hours, a qualified technician would insert the device and, for a nominal fee, hook the user up to the network. Users chose the channels they wished to participate in and connected with fellow PAT users in the area.

Miles intruded on my thoughts. "Mahia, dear, we really do need you to pay attention."

When all I did was shift my position on the couch to turn toward the table and scowl, Miles leaned back in his chair and glared at Cain. "What did you do to her?"

"None of your business," Cain snapped.

"But it is. I don't care what you two get up to in private, although there's more than enough speculation over that charming Darquet blood you have running through you…"

Cain leaned forward, lips pulled back in a snarl as Miles spoke.

"But I need her focused. My message must be delivered."

"Fine," I said as I got up then went to sit at the table with them. The image of the three people he'd electrocuted flashed through my head. If he could kill the captain and her two men without batting an eyelash, I didn't know what else was he capable of.

"Good girl," Miles murmured.

If it had been anyone but Miles, I would have punched them. "Lunar 5, that's what you two were gossiping over?" I asked to get Miles back on track.

"Lunar 5, the fifth colony of the Original Twelve Consortium. I assume you're up to date on its history?" Miles asked me.

I nodded and glanced over at Cain. He had the look of being slightly more in control at least. And "slightly" meant maybe two percent better.

"The Consortium was founded by the twelve families who funded the first commercial base on Original Luna," I said, "in time setting up thirteen other bases on various moons. Excellent bases for incoming business, commercial or otherwise, for the controlling parties of the moon's planet."

"Excellent. Lunar 5 is under the control of the Ayad family, one of the few who maintain two neutral zones," Miles said.

"Neutral zones?"

"Areas where factions or diplomats may meet with no repercussions. Weapons aren't allowed. Neither are credit transactions. No bribes. No fighting," Cain explained.

"Why haven't I heard of that? Original Luna doesn't have those," I said. That sounded like a good idea to me.

Miles shrugged. "Expensive to maintain, and if you decide to use a neutral zone, you've got to have absolute trust in your host."

"Why?"

"Someone has to maintain the peace, keep the order so no one tries anything underhanded. So the host frequently—"

"Blackmails," I interjected. "Of course. Makes sense. If you have to use a neutral zone, it's probably because you're desperate and can't meet up in the usual channels. Or you're criminals looking to make deals. So the host—in this case, the Ayad family—what, tags you? Hangs on to your image and info?"

"Clever." Miles grinned. "I frequently have job openings, if you're ever interested."

I blushed and had to look away. "Um, thanks. But I'm good."

"Pity." Miles sighed. "You'll be meeting with the Star Eaters in the Khepri neutral zone. I recommend arriving early. The sunsets there are quite beautiful."

"No. Arrange the meetup in another location," Cain said. "No tags."

"No can do. Meeting info has already been sent, received, and verified. Any hint of impropriety or shenanigans, and the Star Eaters are likely to get spooked," Miles said with a shake of his head. "But no worries—the Ayads owe me a few."

"Wait. If weapons and such aren't allowed," I asked, ignoring Cain's objections, "how are they supposed to retrieve their message? I'm assuming that kind of equipment won't be allowed."

"Again, the job offer is open," Miles began. "But you're right. No. This just confirms you are carrying the message. Formalities. You are who you say you are and so forth. The Star Eaters will give you directions after that."

"And they know about your little timetable for all this?" I asked.

"I'm assuming they do," Miles responded with a shrug.

"Too risky," Cain said as he pushed away from the table. "Better to take our chances with disarming your bots than play along with your little games."

"Come, now. You should know better than that." Miles began to stand.

I beat him to the punch and reached out to stop him. "It's my deal to make or break. Not his."

Miles threw me a wide grin, his crimson-stained teeth once again reminding me of the horror he'd so easily created on the docking platform. No doubt, that was the point.

<No,> Cain thought.

<Oh, so now you're talking to me?>

I turned to Cain. "Look. I do have a connection to the Star Eaters. We both know that."

"And it would appear Miles has a better understanding of that than I do," he growled.

"Whatever." I rolled my eyes. "Besides, I'm the messenger, for Pluto's sake. I'm the damned message. I'm doing this." *<With or without you.>* I sent the thought before I understood the ramifications of those four words.

Cain's eyes widened, and his tail whipped back and forth behind his legs. He ran a hand through his hair, increasingly long for lack of a proper barber. When he finally looked back at me, his eyes were a dull violet. "If that's what you want."

I needed someone to come scoop my jaw off the floor. I'd been expecting a fight, some kind of pushback.

Surely, he knew that I wasn't just going to let him die, that what I meant was I would keep his annoying self alive with or without his help.

We were strung out on thin atmosphere, but I hadn't expected his look of defeat, that he would quietly sit there and let the countdown run out. But then again, that was his pattern. When I got defensive and pushed at him, he shut down or left. Everyone around me seemed to have that habit.

"Is there anything else you need?" I whirled around and asked Miles, digging my fingernails into my palms as I worked to keep the tears at bay.

Thank Saturn's rings, the man wasn't a total piece of oblivious space junk. "No."

"Great," I croaked, turned, and left.

9

A Little Cardio Exercise

I left Miles's quarters with emotions tumbling down around me, almost suffocating me. Instead of heading back to our assigned room, I turned and headed in the opposite direction. I wondered why I'd allowed myself to get tangled up in that mess. I barely knew Cain, yet I was about to wail like a newborn baby. *But are these tears really for him? Or more for me?*

I only knew that I couldn't return to our room. I needed some time to myself, to sort through the con-flicting emotions and thoughts all screaming for space in my head. Seeing Cain's crestfallen face wasn't what I needed. I didn't need somebody else disappointed in me.

His look of utter disappointment reminded me too much of people's faces right after I'd been released from IGJ custody. Some people had raged and hated me, but those were easy to handle. The problem was the faces who'd spent a little bit of time getting to know me then, upon learning the truth, being devastated that they'd wasted that time.

I hacked my way into another hab-unit on the

opposite side of the deck. No one stopped me. A few times, I froze and held my breath, sure Cain was standing on the other side of the door. But if he was, he never knocked or barged in to demand an explanation. I was sure Miles was sitting behind a monitor somewhere, gleefully chowing down on popcorn and watching the little soap opera play out.

Who cares? Not me.

The next two days went by in a blur, literally and figuratively.

Sleep became increasingly elusive, and the cold sweats switched to nightmares. Disturbing images of my father manipulating, desecrating, or maniacally chuckling over the corpses tucked away in the *Rapscallion*—not to mention the horrific images of Triton suspended in the giant tube, eyes snapping open, and the creepy dead zombie man climbing out of his tomb and coming after me in revenge for his mother's death.

Sleep really isn't a necessary thing, is it?

I hadn't shed so many tears since learning my father had been arrested and I was hauled into the IGJ for questioning.

I felt as if a dam inside me had broken. I sat curled up on the bed and cried over my humiliation at Mrs. Gol's deceit. Tears poured down my face for the shame I no longer denied.

I'd hidden my last name for many years but secretly believed it could still mean something. But after seeing the horror show on the *Rapscallion*, I knew I'd been wrong all along. I'd wasted too many years with a fugitive belief in my father. I'd never known him. When I looked in the mirror, all I could see was another disappointed face staring back. *Who am I?* The question rolled through my head, and I wondered how much of my father's actions formed the core of who I was. The larger implication haunted me. *Was I an innocent victim of Wats Hawking Orion, or did the sins of a parent lie on the shoulders of their children?*

I found no answers for my raging questions. The one potential space for comfort had turned and shown me his disappointment. I was nothing, no one.

When the tears were gone and my body couldn't physically handle being curled up into a tight little ball, I got up and paced. But even the decent amount of room in the hab-unit wasn't enough. So I paced through the ship. No one stopped me. They just ducked their eyes when I headed their way, hurrying about their business.

I bounded downstairs to one of the lower decks with two of the larger cargo holds. The deck had become a favorite place to pace due to the lack of personnel I would have to dodge in my sleep-deprived, emotional-soup-filled haze.

As the calm of the area settled around me, my brain turned toward the too-many questions, what-ifs, and worse-case scenarios that wouldn't leave me alone. *What if Miles suddenly changes his mind about the terms? Or about the deal itself?* Crazy crime bosses did that type of switcheroo. *Would he activate Cain's nanobots for fun?* I had no doubt that possibility was floating around in Miles's mind. *Or what if the meeting with the Star Eaters goes horribly wrong?* My connection with the cult was tenuous at best.

Sure, the crazy cult guys had helped in their own cryptic way with Mrs. Gol and had slipped me the t-square with the warning, but I didn't know anything about them. *How are they organized? Are they a cohesive group? Are there different factions within the Star Eaters who believe or act differently?*

Despite being deep in the pit of despair, I registered a hunched-over figure in front of me and managed to change course in time to avoid them. But the lump stood and stepped out in front of me. It was the same man who'd escorted Cain and me to our room.

"Watch yourself," the man growled.

"Watch myself? You're the one who stepped in my way," I said as I tried to sidestep around him.

Instead of letting me pass, he planted himself in front of me again and crossed his arms against his chest. "No. You're in my way."

Annoyed, I said, "Get lost." I wasn't in the mood for whatever was happening. Once more, I tried to move around the irritating man, but he reached out, spun me around, and pinned me up against the wall.

"You Orion scum," he said, "always thinking you can just do whatever you want."

That was decidedly not what I was expecting.

"Oh, I know who you are. Traitor for a father and a piece of filth for a brother."

"My brother?" The words were slow and sluggish in my mouth.

"Worked for him a couple of years back. Wanna see how he rewards his faithful?" The man shifted so that his left hand pressed against my neck while his other hand reached up to unzip his flight suit.

Confusion, angst, fear, trepidation, worry—all that

was coursing inside me. I felt like a cloud jumper hocked up on stim-pills. I lifted a leg to try to give him a good swift kick in the tenders, but he managed to hook my leg with a foot and pinned it against the wall.

"This is what my devotion got me," he snarled as he pulled the zipper down to his waist, reached up, and tugged down on the collar of his shirt.

Horrific burns coated his skin—thick, calloused scars of knotted flesh.

He leaned forward. "Tell me why I shouldn't visit the same on his sister."

What do you get when you mix a lack of sleep, a world turned upside down, and a whole host of crazy emotions? One white blazing ball of fury. That reminds me: if you haven't seen a supernova, I suggest you book tickets with the Surio Science Observatory and Research Center. It's worth the money and travel time to witness such a wonder. Right after my release from IGJ custody, I'd booked a ticket and fled civilization, definitely something I wished to do at this moment.

I slammed a hand against the wrist holding on to my neck, and before the man knew what was happening, I rammed an elbow into his head. He stumbled back, dazed from the sudden onslaught.

"Try it," I snarled. Perhaps inviting violence wasn't the right answer, but I'd had enough. And doing it felt good.

The man shook his head and spat at me, "Not worth the effort."

"Yeah? I think you're a coward," I said, sneering.

His face turned beet red, and his hands moved to his tool belt.

"Bring it on, big boy," I snarled, crouching and ready for a fight.

"I think the lady has had enough," someone called out in a calm voice. "It would be wise for you to go back to work."

We both looked over at the stairs to see Miles casually leaning against the railing.

"Enjoying the show?" I snapped. "Wanna take bets?"

"Another time, perhaps," he said. "You, find another deck to work."

The man hesitated, but only for a fraction of a second. "Yes, sir." He snapped a salute, picked up his tools, and left.

"I could've taken him," I said.

Miles finished coming down the stairs and stared at me. "I do believe you could have. But what did I tell you about leaking?"

I didn't care who Miles was or what he was capable of. I was furious, and all my balled-up emotions needed an outlet. I rushed the man—not my finest hour.

Miles stepped to the side, and I slammed into the stairs. With a snarl, I spun around and rushed toward him again. That time, he stood his ground. I threw my all into a strong right hook but swung wide, and Miles threw a check hook with his left fist and caught me right on the edge of my cheekbone.

I felt the impact but didn't care. With a few hops, I regained my balance and moved my arms up into a defensive position. My right arm rotated and shot straight out as I stepped forward. Miles caught the jab and my subsequent cross with ease.

"Is this all you have?" he asked as though we were sipping wine and playing croquet.

I threw myself at him with my fists swinging out of control, but my brief moment of uncontrolled rage burned too quickly. Miles caught my wrists and let me sink into a sobbing mess on the deck floor—definitely not one of my finer moments.

"Does everyone hate the Orions? We weren't all bad. Or has everything just been a lie? My father and now Jupiter only knows what with my brother…" I looked up and glared at Miles. "I've been a fool this whole time, thinking if I kept my head down, everything would be fine. Not great or grand but at least fine. I had a job, and I had my own place. I had control. Now? Now, what do I have?"

<You have me.>

Miles gave me one last look before he turned and quietly walked up the stairs as Cain came down, which left the two of us alone.

"No, I don't," I stubbornly muttered. "You'll use me then leave. Just like they did. You've already proved that."

Undignified as it was, I tried to crawl away from him. Literally. My legs were as wobbly as jelly, the traitors. Yet Cain reached out and pulled me toward him so that we were sitting in a tangled mess on the floor.

"I know. And I apologize," he whispered.

That simple word held so much weight—not just from Cain but in general.

Apologize. Apology. Forgiveness. Words I'll never hear from…

I realized that somewhere between leaving the *Starshine* and staying on Epsilon's Station, I had switched from using the more intimate, loving moniker of Pops to the distant, formal title of father. My subconscious had distanced itself from the man before I'd understood what it was doing.

As I sat there, no longer fighting against Cain, I let that realization sink in.

Pops had been a cheerful, loving, and kind man, bursting with information on obscure relics and cultures. My father was a mystery, a man I didn't understand, someone I didn't like, who could do horrific things and kill people without a second thought.

I wondered if I would ever get Pops back again.

"What we are, what we could be is… complicated," Cain said as the fog lifted from my brain.

"All I want is trustworthy," I mumbled.

<I can do that.>

I twisted around and stared at him. "Can you? You're really not great at sharing information."

Cain stared at me. He didn't look away, and I watched, mesmerized, as his irises shifted from violet to amber, a dazzling, sparkling, crystallized amber.

"There was a time when I shared too much, and it almost cost me everything." His words were soft but sincere. "Heart stones are protected by the males in a Darquet family. I—" Cain looked down then back at me, shame coating his face. "It took several years of wearing my grandfather down, but he eventually shared the secrets of our family's heart stone."

Realization of what Cain was confessing washed over me. "You told your sister, didn't you?"

He nodded. "It was before our father became so ill.

Elea can pass for a full-blooded Darquet, and I can't. One day, after training with some other diplomat's children and an excellent amount of remarks about my mixed blood, I needed to prove I was as much a Dar as Elea looked.

"I burst into her room and made a few unkind comments about how she might look like a Darquet, but I was the real Darquet because I'd been told the location of our family's heart stone."

His reluctance to tell me his plans suddenly made sense. If he didn't tell me, then I couldn't run off half-cocked on my own and get in trouble.

"Besides, you have a habit of not wanting to follow my orders. What would you do if I just handed you everything I knew? Would you take off and try to fix it yourself? Like Elea did?" Cain added.

I guessed he had a point. *Maybe…*

"Why do you care?" I mumbled.

Cain pulled me close, and I tucked my head under his chin.

<*You're my heart's blood.*>

"What's that supposed to mean?" I asked, trying not to whine.

<*It's complicated. Truly. And I don't even understand it myself. When you have time, look up the Darquet myth of Itheron and Lia.*>

I pulled back a little to look at him. "Don't you think we've got enough puzzles to solve?"

He chuckled. "I thought you enjoyed history."

I lightly tapped him on the arm and curled up against

him. We sat there for a long time, long enough that I was lulled to sleep by the gentle rhythm of his heartbeat.

I woke to find that Cain must have carried me back to our room and curled up beside me on the bed. My eyes burned, and my mouth was dry. I wish I could say my sleep had been peaceful. Instead, my mind insisted on replaying the same image of Cain, standing in the middle of Epsilon Station's main terminal, his amber eyes sadly watching me as I walked away.

"You know I won't let you die," I mumbled.

<I know. I was caught off guard.>

"I'm sorry," I whispered.

My thoughts tumbled over each other, and I didn't mean to let the thought slip out. *<What if I can't learn how to trust?>*

"We'll learn to trust and accept together," he murmured as his lips brushed against my forehead. A pleasant chill shot down my spine, and that time, I fell into a deep, untroubled sleep.

10

Buy the Nose Pinchers...
Trust Me

For what was left of our time on board the *Whimsy*, I slept. Admittedly, it wasn't much, but when Cain roused me to say we'd made it to Lunar 5, I felt better than I had since we left the *Rapscallion*, minus the whole countdown to doom.

Before we made our escape from the crazed leader of the Little Asteroids, he was waiting for us on the ship's cargo ramp. Miles launched into a grand recounting of the numerous credits he'd shelled out in order to bribe our way through the increased checkpoints around Lunar 5. One would think he was angling for an award or something by the way he went on and on.

"I've secured rooms at Rio Latte." He fixed an eye on Cain. "Just your style."

With Cain's grimace, I wasn't sure how to interpret that statement.

"And you, little lady." Miles turned toward me. "Don't forget our deal. The meet and greet is set for nine tomorrow evening. Khepri neutral zone. Check in and get comfortable. No loitering about. No leakage. And mind the timetable. Clear?"

I nodded as anticipation bubbled up inside. *<We made it.>*

<Don't get eager just yet.>

We'd finally gotten to Lunar 5, where the IGJ had discovered Jorge's body, the place that might provide the answers we both needed. I think I was entitled to a little bit of anticipation.

I was walking down the ramp toward the decontamination zone when I realized Cain hadn't followed. I stopped and turned. He and Miles were still talking. And I'd thought the Orion family was bad about getting lost down verbal wormholes.

I knew Cain and I had talked about trust and all that jazz, but nobody just turns over a new leaf in a few days. Curiosity and concern won out, and I edged back up the ramp.

"And the Tretoono Club?" Cain was asking.

"Add it to the list of what you owe me. The Triplets and I made a deal. It'll hold." Miles grinned, and not in a neighborly, good-to-see-you way. "For now."

Miles leaned forward and whispered. Cain's tail twitched, and his lips pulled back to reveal his impressively sharp canines.

"One day, your highness," Cain replied with a snarl.

Miles pulled away. "If you survive the rest of the week, your eminence,"—he finished with a flourish and a bow—"you can find me at the Emerald Oasis."

Cain turned and stalked down the ramp. His hand

shot out, grabbed my arm, and towed me along with him.

"What was that about?" I asked.

His fingers dug into my arm, making his simmering rage palpable. "An old blood debt between us. One of these days, it must be paid."

That was far more information than I'd expected, and with our newly minted truce or agreement—honestly, I didn't know what it was—all I said was "Huh."

The decontamination zone was standard—we stripped down, got sprayed, and waited to be scanned. We had to rinse and repeat until the authorities were satisfied. Having spent so much time in the absolutely upstanding environment of Epsilon's Station, Cain and I were decontaminated three times.

We passed through security without a hitch, and no one mentioned the bots crawling around inside us. Either Miles had paid this zone off as well, or the bots didn't register on their sensors.

Lunar 5 and its sibling bases were all built using the same blueprints. That meant, having lived on Original Luna, I knew my way around Lunar 5. The sensation of knowing I was someplace new but feeling everything as familiar was a bit of a letdown. Not even the déjà vu sent a tingle of excitement down my spine. Traveling around as a kid had prepped my brain for craving the new and exciting, and the events of the past few weeks had rejuvenated that part of me.

The base's design was simple. Each lunar base was divided into four districts: commercial, residential, recreational, and administrative. The stately spires of the administrative offices were located at the heart of the base, towering over everything else and separated from the other three districts with a heavily guarded wall an impressive four and a half meters high.

The layout reminded me of a of pie. And that made me hungry.

Anyway, all incoming and outgoing ships, transports, cargo haulers, and personally registered vehicles had only one choice of docking ports in the commercial district. Access was regularly monitored.

Toward the west of the commercial district, the buildings tapered and gave way to residential. The buildings in residential, which butted up against the commercial district, started with short-term housing and gradually moved to long-term options.

Moving through the residential area, we eventually wound our way to the recreational district. The area was complete with gyms, holostores, adrenaline-junkie adventures, and the greens, which butted up against long-term residential areas.

"We should go check in," I said.

At the same time, Cain stated, "We should scout out the Khepri neutral zone."

"That wasn't a part of our instructions."

"You're going to follow his instructions?" Cain asked suspiciously.

"He is a madman, after all." I tried not to, but my hand flew to my arm where Miles had injected me. "Besides, I'm hungry." The mouthwatering thought of pie wouldn't go away.

"You're always hungry," Cain muttered.

"Am not." I didn't know why he would say such a thing. "We can grab food, check into our rooms, then scout out the Khepri neutral zone."

"What if it's a—"

"Trap?" I finished. "After all this time, the expense, personally escorting us here, you think now he's going to spring a trap on us?"

"You're the one who keeps telling me he's mad," Cain retorted then muttered, "and you don't know the half of it."

I shivered at that. I was curious about how Cain knew someone like Miles, but I didn't want to know badly enough to ask, not yet. Watching true-crime dramas was one thing, but being up close and personal was another. And I wasn't sure how much more my brain could take of horrific images of death and torture.

Unfortunately, I would find out.

But not until after I ate a rather pleasant meal at Space Fried Quid. Intergalactic fast-food chain, better than one would think—they even offered pie. Imagine that.

And not before we checked into the room at Rio Latte, a swank and undoubtedly expensive accommodation for Miles to book for us. Our door had a Certified Fresh tag, and I couldn't find a hint of any dermatex. Plus, the room even came with a complimentary breakfast. I supposed Cain, the child of a diplomat, had grown accustomed to a certain standard, and for the life of me, I couldn't figure out why the Rio Latte wouldn't be a good fit. Maybe he just didn't like the thought of Miles making the arrangements.

Adequately stuffed to the point that I couldn't think

about taking another bite of food, we headed off to scope out the Khepri neutral zone. But we had to take a bit of a detour when we ran into a rather large crowd. A pop-up store was a bit of a surprise in the middle of the residential district. After we earned our fair share of frowns, elbows, and unkind, unrepeatable words, I stopped to ask what was going on.

An older man turned, looked me up and down, and sniffed with a fair amount of disdain. "Spacer, eh? Wait your turn. Those of us living here have been waiting for our upgrades ever since they closed down the first processing center."

I frowned. "What?"

"The best tech around." The man scoffed with a shake of his head.

That was a part of Confore's infomercials, with some catchy tune singing their praises.

"What's the upgrade?" Cain asked.

"The SeeClear tech," the man replied. "Supposed to have gotten that upgrade when it was rolled out to everyone else, see? But no, someone had to go and botch up the delivery. Shut 'em down at the docks, then force us to wait. Can't trust the lot of them."

I was still glad I hadn't subscribed to the whole bioupgrade fads, and I wanted to ask the man a few questions about his feelings over the SeeClear implants. Before leaving on my vacation—if it could still be called that—I'd fielded several calls over shipping issues and bugs in the tech. Heck, I might've even talked with this guy. Cain's fingers wrapped around my arm.

<But maybe I can help,> I protested.

<No.>

Cain tightened his grip and pulled me along, probably because he could feel a tirade of help desk stories brewing. After pushing through the crowds, we made it to the Khepri neutral zone, which turned out to be one of the greens.

Too much time had passed since I'd had a chance to relish actual living things from Earth. I wanted to spend some time soaking it all in, but Cain was all business and no pleasure.

<You could do infomercials for the IGJ.>

Cain turned and frowned. "What?"

"The way you're standing there, all important and official," I said. To prove my point, I puffed out my chest, planted my fists on my hips, and turned my head to look up toward the artificial sky.

<I don't look like that.>

I chuckled, moved to a different spot, and changed my position, placing one hand on an imaginary holstered gun at my hip, my other arm relaxed at my side. Then I fixed as serious a gaze as I could on Cain.

But the combination of his signature scowl and immediate attempt to not stand in any way, shape, or form like what I'd imitated caused me to burst out laughing.

Cain's tail snapped back and forth, and he turned his back on me. When he was satisfied with whatever he'd been doing, he marched past me.

<Coming?>

"Oh yes, great and protective IGJ man," I called out.

Cain's shoulders stiffened, but he didn't turn around and just kept on walking.

Hey, if I couldn't add a bit of levity to a pretty tense situation, then I didn't know what life was for. In reality, I was nervous. *Terrified* was a more adequate word—terrified of losing the budding relationship with Cain, that something would go wrong, or that Miles would decide to get things over with and see Cain dead. I didn't care about meeting up with the Star Eaters. That was merely a small bump in the road to unraveling Jorge's mystery.

We did take our time heading back to the hotel, and Cain eventually slowed down to let me catch up. The silence between us wasn't uncomfortable, and instead of lingering irritation, I sensed a touch of amusement from the man.

The evening at Rio Latte was calm and uneventful, and Cain settled into one of the moderately cushy recliners while I sprawled out on the bed.

"We would have time to do some looking around tomorrow before meeting up with the Star Eaters," I commented.

"That's not a part of Miles's instructions," Cain quipped.

I looked over at him and shrugged. "Technically, we've followed his instructions. We checked in. We're comfortably settled into our room. And loitering means to stand around or hang out somewhere without a purpose." I rolled over and grinned. "We would be disobeying his instructions if we loitered around the hotel all day tomorrow, waiting for the meeting. If we move about Lunar 5 with a purpose, then we're not loitering."

Cain laughed, deep and rich, which sent shivers down

my skin. I made a mental note to try to make him laugh more often.

"Fill me in about Jorge and the IGJ," I said.

Cain gave me the rundown on the man's service record. Jorge Silone-Ruger had worked for the Inter-Galactic Justice system for thirty-three years, a few years above average. His rating was high enough to give him access to midlevel classified reports, and all his evaluations scored high in interpersonal relationships, marksmanship, voluntary educational boosts, and risk management. The only area marked with a need for improvement was record keeping.

Not helpful, Jorge. Not helpful.

Jorge had never married, and no public record of any children existed. He had a sister, but she'd died during the famines on Old Earth at the end of the Cricade Wars.

I picked up Jorge's biography when it came to his time at Confore. It amounted to very little. I knew Jorge had worked three floors above me in the engineering development department, but that was all. Guessing what tech lines Confore was developing or working on was above my security clearance.

"If Confore is engaged in illicit trading outside of sanctioned areas, I don't understand why Jorge wasn't placed in marketing or accounting," I said. "Unless it has to do with the fact he's human? It's not like the Weplies go out of their way to hire non-Weplies. Frankly, I'm still amazed I was interviewed, let alone hired."

Cain gave me a thoughtful look, "Why were you hired?"

And we're changing the subject.

"Jorge got a job in development. So perhaps it really doesn't have anything to do with illicit trading," I said.

A tinge of curiosity seeped through our telepathic connection at my deft evasion of his question, but I was grateful he didn't push the subject.

"What's the biggest tech push on the market right now? With Confore?" Cain asked.

That I could answer. "The SeeClear hardware update. What that man was talking about. Confore had a grav-dump of a time with issues on the 3.0 model. Went to work on developing the 3.5 patches right away. That was roughly…" I frowned as I thought back through the heaps of calls I'd gotten at the help desk. "Three months ago. They've continued to push deeply dis-counted updates and bonus add-ons to entice everyone to upgrade."

Cain straightened in his chair. "I've seen ads for the tech. Never considered it myself, with all the add-ons through the IGJ."

I nodded. "Yup. The 3.5 upgrades have been pushed hard. I didn't consider it—" I sat up and gave Cain an incredulous look. "You don't think it'd be that easy, do you?"

He frowned. "What?"

"SeeClear. Project Clear Sight?"

His frown deepened, and this time, he was the one who got up and paced back and forth. "A bit obvious, even for the IGJ. But you toss in an unimaginative agent, and I could see them taking the name and run-ning with it."

"Confore's push of the 3.5 upgrades, paired with

Jorge getting a job on the engineering development floor, would all line up," I said.

"It would. And it does." Cain moved from his chair to sit next to me on the bed. "And would account for why the Jumjul weren't contacted."

"Minus the idea of a larger conspiracy. Or the IGJ beginning to push back against the Jumjul," I muttered.

"Right," Cain said with a long sigh.

He ran a hand through his hair, giving his head a quick scratch. I was beginning to believe I liked how the longer hair looked on him. *A tad bit more rugged. A little rough and… Man, I've got to stop.*

"There is a small but increasing movement away from Jumjul authority," Cain said, interrupting my line of thinking.

"Risky, isn't it? Who would be crazy enough to go up against the Jumjul?"

Cain's mood shifted.

"What aren't you saying?" I asked.

Cain dodged my question. "Have you been keeping up with recent political whispers?"

"Are you subtly trying to ask me if I subscribe to the whisper nets? Do you really think I'm the type of person who would listen to that garbage? After featuring heavily on several of the channels for years?"

I watched him struggle with a way to answer my questions diplomatically.

The whisper nets were the guilty pleasure for a majority of individuals, judging by the numerous channels and subscriber ratios. But they were also the breeding ground for conspiracy theorists and nutjobs. However,

I didn't just take what governments and bureaucrats touted as fact. They lie and are underhanded, just like black market runners.

There's a lot of strange stuff out there in the universe. Mix that up with hundreds of species, unique cultural backgrounds, religions, myths, and hang-ups, and you've got the ripest, most foul-smelling piece of kitho fruit you've ever tasted. And if you've never tasted it, you should. Just make sure to wear a pair of nose pinchers. The worse the smell, the riper the fruit.

I'll never forget my first piece of kitho. I hadn't been on Original Luna long and kept trying different spots to eat, including one little hole-in-the-wall Nezgathi-run fruit stall tucked away on the edge of where the commercial district met the residential. The stink from the place initially drove me away, but every time I passed, I kept seeing customers flocking to the place—not just Nezgathi, with their limited olfactory senses, but humans, Neethos, and even a few Weplies.

I decided to give it a try. Of course, I didn't want to spring for the extra nose pinchers. I was going to eat the fruit, not sniff it. Oh boy, did I ever learn my lesson there. If you survive the initial gag reflux and can hold out for the aftertaste, it's the sweetest thing you've ever tasted. If you ever get the chance, I recommend you check it out.

Just get the nose pinchers, all right?

Anyway, the whisper nets were a hotbed of conspiracy theorists and the poor saps who believed every word, not to mention the vitriol most channels spewed about my father. On the flip side, I had no doubt the tales I could spin myself might line up with those of some of the channel's theorists.

"No," I finally answered. "I don't."

Relief washed across his face. "It's a requirement with the IGJ. An easy way to feel the pulse of current trends and shifts."

"So, what are you trying to hint at?" I asked.

Cain shifted his weight, and his tail rustled in the sheets. "The Eeri."

I stared at him. "What about those cloud suckers?"

"There are rumors a few of the governments might be considering new agreements with the Eeri… in exchange for pushing back the Jumjul."

11

And the Plot Thickens…
into a Lumpy Mess

"You've got to be kidding." I meant it.

I shared in the collective animosity toward the Eeri. Due to the damage and lives lost, the Cricade Wars would go down as one of the worst conflicts in human history, not to mention my obvious personal reasons for not liking the species.

I was holding on to the notion that my father must've had a noble reason for doing what he did, and to be truthful, I'm not sure I was wrong. Whatever Mrs. Gol had hinted at, a shady group of tattooed nutjobs—yes, I was lumping my father into that group—was definitely worth stopping.

Hey, Pops, was dealing with the Eeri, betraying your own species, worth it? Can you send me some cosmic answer to that? Hub, Mr. Big Shot I'm Just Going to Leave My Kids with No Explanation? Was there no other way?

To my disappointment, I didn't receive an answer—no

searing lightning bolt, no sudden voice through the Sur-T Screen in the room.

"They would be trading one overlord for another," I muttered.

"I agree. But the channels are increasing and so is the chatter," Cain said.

"Think that's why the IGJ didn't involve the Jumjul? Are they trying to play both sides?"

Cain shook his head. "No, more like trying to stay neutral. There's a lot of talk internally, scare tactics and the like. But no matter what you might believe, the IGJ doesn't want to be caught in the middle. No way to keep doing their job if that happens."

I snorted. "Right. The IGJ is the good guy."

Cain scowled. "On the whole, they are."

He could believe what he wanted. That was a topic I doubted we would ever see eye to eye on.

"All right. So Jorge was potentially investigating the SeeClear hardware push. Still, could fall into the idea of illicit trading. Something hinky with the tech."

<Hinky?>

I sniffed. *<Don't mock my word choices.>*

"If there was something… hinky with the tech, wouldn't you know? Help desk lady?" Cain asked.

His eyes definitely held a spark of something mischievous, a small crack in his gruff, exterior shell. I liked it.

I considered this question. "Despite Confore's stance on a hundred percent satisfaction guarantee and no host-rejection issues, the help desk was still fielding a large volume of frustrated customers. Think

Confore thought I knew something because of all the calls I took? I'm not the only one who works the help desk, though."

"But you're the only other human at the company."

And we were back to that pesky little detail. Weplies did protect their own. But to be fair, most species did. Ingrained biases could be challenging to spot and break through.

"What were the majority of complaints about?" Cain asked.

With a deep breath, I tried to refresh my memory. "Glitches, faulty hardware. System reboots and, in some cases, blindness."

"Anything stand out?"

I shook my head. "No. One thing I learned while working for tech companies is that there are always issues. Nothing ever has all the bugs worked out, and no one can ever predict how one piece of tech might interact with another, especially with biotech."

I frowned. "But I don't see how that has any relevance to chatter over a new deal with the cloud suckers."

"Neither do I." Cain scowled as he brushed some of his hair back out of his face. "What we need to ascertain is why Jorge ended up here on Lunar 5."

"Where do you suggest we start?"

"Where they found his body."

"Great. Thanks, Captain Obvious, and where was that?" I asked sweetly.

"Docking Platform Nineteen."

I leaned back against the wall. "You've never shared his autopsy report. How was he killed?"

"Inconclusive."

I frowned. "Not helpful, then."

Cain nodded. "No. But just because no foul play was discovered, doesn't mean Jorge wasn't murdered. There's more than a handful of ways to kill someone and leave no trace."

"So tomorrow, we check out Docking Platform Nineteen. Plenty of time to look around before meeting up with the Star Eaters," I said.

Cain nodded. "But before all that, you should get some rest."

"As should you. I've got a bad feeling tomorrow is going to be a long day."

<You and me both.>

Cain stood, and I couldn't help but watch as he shrugged off his jacket and neatly folded it up for a makeshift pillow. His undershirt was well tailored for his compact musculature, and the image of him without it flashed through my mind. I eyed the chair, and a different type of anxiety balled up inside me.

When I hadn't been on a sleep-deprived tear through the *Whimsy* and Cain and I had shared a hab-unit, he'd graciously slept on the hard, flat chair in the room. I eyeballed this room's chair. Granted, it appeared a lot more comfortable, but that didn't mean he needed to continue to try to sleep in a chair.

"We could share?" I suggested, my voice a little higher and shakier than I wanted.

Cain had his back to me as he was arranging his jacket-cum-pillow, and he froze. I caught a ripple of muscle underneath his shirt.

<The offer is appreciated. But this is best.>

I really wasn't offering anything more than simply sharing the most comfortable place in the room to lie down and get a good night's sleep. *Honestly… well, mostly. I think. Oh, I don't know.*

I felt a bit deflated at his polite refusal of my offer.

Cain turned, and the stare he fixed on me made me blush from head to toe.

<I'm not rejecting you. Quite the opposite.>

"Okay," I squeaked and kept silent as he finished getting ready to sleep.

Ultimately, he was right. Neither one of us needed any more complications, and for the first time in a long time, I knew my relationship with Cain had the potential to be something far different than most ever had a chance to experience.

Neither one of us spoke the rest of the evening. I stretched out, balling up the top cover for a wall of support to my right, and stacked two of the pillows together. With my left arm tucked up under the pillows, I watched as Cain worked to find the most comfortable position that sleeping curled up in a chair would allow.

A bundle of directly conflicting emotions was attached to that man—dreams best left to the imagination and real-life moments I would never have expected after his fateful attempt to flash his badge at the charging horde of tiny Glipglows. All that mixed with his occasionally vexing attitude. But Cain was offering something far beyond mere physical companionship. And as I drifted off to sleep, I wondered if I would be brave enough to fully accept it.

12

My Very Own Walking Encyclopedia

According to the clock embedded in the wall, it was midmorning when Cain woke me up.

<*Five more minutes,*> I whined.

"I'll grab breakfast if you get up," he whispered.

I opened one eye then the other and muttered, "Fine."

Drowsy and already feeling apprehensive over what the day might bring, I stumbled to my feet as Cain left.

Honestly, I appreciated the few moments alone. I needed time to sort through a jumbled mess of theories, ideas, and concerns as I washed up and got ready. But rather than making any progress in organizing the mental mess, I only succeeded in tying my stomach up in a few more knots.

My biggest concern was the damned nanobots in Cain's blood, merrily waiting to go boom in their fifteen minutes of fame. If the Star Eaters didn't uphold their end of the deal, I wasn't sure how I was going to convince Miles that wasn't our fault. I wasn't sure he would care anyway.

By the time I finished, Cain returned. He took a seat in his chair, and I eyeballed a nefarious brown lump in his hand.

"I thought we got complimentary breakfast. Shouldn't that be a bit more than a—" My words fell away before Cain's grin.

He pointed at the neatly made bed, where a bright-red platter with an accompanying cover sat on a wooden tray. I wasn't sure what impressed me more, the implied hint of a sumptuous breakfast hidden beneath the silver scrollwork-embellished dish cover or the fact that Cain had made the bed. The *Whimsy* hadn't had enough of a bed for Cain to do much, and I, for one, never wasted time making beds. I didn't see the point since I was simply going to ball the sheets up again into a comfortable nest the next night.

I pulled off the cover, and my mouth instantly watered at a traditional, honest-to-goodness human breakfast: biscuits and gravy, a fried egg, two pieces of dubious-looking bacon, and a small serving of hash browns.

"My favorite," I said, twisting around to look at him. "How did you know?"

Cain shrugged with a mischievous grin and took a bite of his zip.

I hadn't grown up on that type of food. I learned about it through one of the many history lessons my brother and I had suffered through. My father had believed it important that his children knew not only the general history of whatever species we were interacting with but our own history as well, our ancestry.

Those lessons had extended back into the mid-twentieth century. When we went through lessons centered around food—its cultural importance, societal implications, and regional cuisines—I latched on to one of the countries in Northern Something or Other—I can't recall the name—for their breakfast, I fell in love with a thing called sushi, and I could never get enough of the spices and flavors from a variety of Middle Eastern countries.

For a significant period of time, I vexed both my father and brother by refusing to eat anything else. Thinking back on it, I wonder how many credits my father shelled out in order to feed me during that particular phase.

I plopped down on the bed and dug in.

"Good?" Cain asked.

"Definitely," I said around a mouthful of hash browns.

Cain finished his breakfast far more quickly than I did and switched on the Sur-T Screen to pull up a map of Lunar 5. He focused on the commercial zone and zoomed in. "Docking Platform Nineteen," he pointed out.

I took my food with me and stood next to him. "Everything looks standard to me. No additional security checkpoints. At least none that are pinged on the map."

"Which may or may not mean anything," Cain said. "But at least it won't take long to get there. We can miss most of the mass transport too. Less chance of triggering a checkpoint."

"Not a lot of faith in Miles and his work at keeping us off the radar?" I asked.

Cain shook his head for an answer.

<Still not going to tell me how the two of you know each other?>

<No.>

I chewed the last of my fried egg, fighting the urge to purposefully say something I knew would hurt—a defensive habit that I was recognizing and trying to own up to. But that was difficult when Cain was withholding information. Trust was a two-way street.

<I can still hear you when you sulk.>

"And I'm still waiting for you to not keep information from me," I snapped. *Whoops.* I still needed to work on my control a bit.

Before Cain could say anything, a flutter of nervous anxiety in my stomach sprang to life as I swallowed my embarrassment and my pride. "Look, all I mean is—"

Cain turned to me, his eyes a vexing mix of emerald and amber. I could see his tension in how his shoulders were thrown back a tad too much and how he clenched his jaw. *<Thank you.>* "There are some aspects of my life to which I'm... I would rather not share quite yet."

Oh, how I wanted to continue to dig at him, to just rip the layers off and figure out what he didn't want exposed. But I held my tongue and said, "Okay."

That was the hardest word I'd spoken in quite some time, something so simple and plain. I didn't speak the word falsely, but it was laced with uncertainty and a fair amount of distrust.

Cain lifted a hand and reached out. For a moment, I thought he was going to run his thumb down my cheek, but his hand stilled in midair for a second before he let it drop back down. "In time, I'll try to explain."

I nodded and turned to set my plate down on the bed. I picked up the cover and stared at the delicate flourish of swirls and intricate patterns and wondered if we would ever untangle ourselves from the complications of our pasts. As I gently set the cover back down on the plate, I found myself fervently hoping we could.

"So off to find the wizard?" I tried to jest. But I didn't feel as carefree as I was trying to sound.

Cain frowned. "What?"

I shook my head, annoyed he didn't understand the reference. "Never mind."

Cain stared at me for a moment, and I would've sworn he wanted to say something, but instead, he gave me a small nod, and without further discussion, we headed off to find Docking Platform Nineteen.

Lunar bases weren't mazes. They were well thought out, with easy access between each district, as were most bases, stations, and colonies. Nobody would want to live or work in a precarious bubble that protected them from the vacuum of space or hostile atmospheres if the architect hadn't thought things through. Emergency situations did happen. That was a fact of colonizing space. Designs that were convoluted and complicated wasted time and lives.

We passed a few security guards at random intervals

on the docks but only received a few curious looks, thankfully. Despite the fair amount of black market trading Lunar 5 allowed, I felt as if we had a neon sign flashing above us, declaring that we were on the IGJ's top-ten list.

I let out a small sigh of relief when we made it to Platform Nineteen without incident. The platform wasn't what I'd expected.

I'd been prepared for a dark space like what had awaited us on Epsilon's Station, perhaps even another ambush. But Lunar 5 maintained well lit, clean, and very spacious platforms. No cargo boxes, tools, or any tidbits of various parts for repair work were scattered around, perhaps to discourage any illicit behavior from an already shady bunch. Or maybe a megalomaniac neat freak was in charge. That could definitely have been an option.

"Looks deserted," Cain commented.

Oh yeah. That was probably a better conclusion than where I was headed. *Sheesh.*

"Then the next question is was this space in use or not when they found Jorge?" I asked.

"Let's take a look."

Cain located one of the comm panels with Lunar 5's logo backlit by an iridescent moon rotating on the dormant screen. With one tap, the screen flared to life with a wide variety of options.

"Per Old Earth Monarchy and the Goldsmith Consortium trade regulations, implemented in conjunction with the Jumjul High Courts, all trading companies, whether in the business of trading material goods or stocks and credits, must legally register with the Jumjul

High Court and maintain their company information for public record," Cain said.

"Great recitation," I commented.

"Trading codex page thirty-three, paragraph two, subsection nine," Cain said with an offhand shrug.

I stared at him. "Perfect recall?"

"Just another perk of IGJ upgrades. You wouldn't believe the number of individuals who try to quote the laws at agents to get out of a jam."

"Great, now I know you're a walking legal book. What fun," I remarked sarcastically.

Cain actually smiled. *Color me purple and shove me out an air lock.*

"There hasn't been a company registered here until about a month ago. Looks like a Glipglow subsidiary of Reloprotuthia."

"That's a mouthful," I muttered.

"Reloprotuthia is the name of the previous den mother." Cain turned to me with a mischievous look. The little upturn to his mouth, the veiled delight in his expression was new, which I liked. "Are you telling me there's a cultural custom you don't know about?"

"Hey," I said with a playful slap on his arm, "not all of us can be walking encyclopedias."

A spark of amber shone in Cain's eyes, and his tail twitched. He took a step toward me, and my cheeks flushed as my face grew hot. He opened his mouth to say something, but for some unknown reason, he stopped himself. The look was gone, and he took two steps back.

To say I was disappointed would be an understatement.

"Den mothers are honored above all else in Glipglow society, even above masters. It's a common custom to name important parts of the culture after a recently passed den mother. A tad confusing at times for non-Glipglows, as the species seem to have an intuitive sense of how to keep everything straight," Cain explained.

I murmured a few *ah*s and *oh*s but really didn't care about the customs of Glipglow culture at the time. My mind was furiously scrambling to figure out if I'd given some type of hint that his attentions were unwelcome. I certainly didn't think I had, but Cain was proceeding with caution, which I did respect.

"Looks like there was a short-term corporation that rented the space before the subsidiary of Reloprotuthia, Opali-Pcli Technological Solutions," Cain noted.

I forced myself back to the task at hand. "Is this comm panel routed into the main database network?"

Cain input a few different queries, then a deep frown settled upon his face. "There's been a massive data purge." He continued to try to access information as he continued, "Every IGJ agent rotates through the different departments, which builds relationships and gives an agent a solid sense of all the moving parts of the IGJ. But it means I recognize this data purge and block. This was done by the IGJ. Top-level clearance work."

"Wouldn't that make sense? The IGJ investigated Jorge's death," I said.

Cain shook his head. "Yes and no. Files can be purged. But the Jumjul High Court frowns upon it. They don't like hidden data. The IGJ has to petition and go through a complicated series of meetings to obtain permission from the Jumjul High Court. And even then, there's supposed to be a summary record left as to why the data purge occurred."

"That's a romantic notion, to maintain a level of transparency, but I can attest our society doesn't work that way. Not in the slightest," I muttered.

Cain shrugged. "The challenge of working with different species—they all have their own cultural and societal norms. The average person can fly under the Jumjul radar. But the IGJ? This is grounds for serious legal action."

"More evidence of moving away from the Jumjul, then?" I asked.

"I don't know." Cain ran a hand through his hair and sounded exasperated. "I'll have to do some digging. But…" He paused as he switched back to the platform-rental information. "Opali-Poli Technological Solutions withdrew their rental a day before Jorge was killed."

"Suspicious timing."

Cain nodded. "It is. And the best lead we've got so far." He backed out of the rental information until Lunar 5's logo returned to the screen. "Does Opali-Poli sound familiar?"

I ran through my memory to see if anything would come up in conjunction with the name. "Well, Opali-Poli was an important religious destination for the Lesser Seeds of Irolo. An obscure religion, there aren't many left who practice it, although there are the converts now and again. The religion was built around the belief of sacrificing the many for the good of the one. A little backward from the majority of religions out there."

"So, a company from the Lesser Seeds?"

"Could be. Who's it registered to?"

"Faraday Insurances," Cain said.

I frowned. "Another name I'm not familiar with. ChowHo is the biggest fish in the insurance pond. The help desk gets misrouted calls about insurance policies all the time. Next up would be Oceanic, Eret Tulin—that's a Wepli-run company—and In-House Solutions."

"Could just be a small start-up business or local trafficker looking to make a quick buck and set up a few dummy groups," Cain surmised.

Of course that was possible, as was the chance that everything could be innocent. But Jorge, whatever he'd been investigating, had come to Lunar 5 for a reason and wound up dead. And now we were suspicious that the IGJ had circumvented Jumjul authority to cover that up.

I saw the deflation in Cain's body language and felt the same disappointment. "As you said, we've at least got a lead now. We've got plenty of time before meeting up with the Star Eaters. Let's find a public comm and see what we can find out about Opali-Poli and Faraday."

<Agreed.>

13

Is a Seeing-Eye Cat
a Thing?

We were wrapped up in our own thoughts, and I waited as Cain poked around a bit more on Docking Platform Nineteen. By the time he was done being an IGJ agent, the hour was well past noon. We had plenty of time to make our evening rendezvous with the Star Eaters, but I was hungry again.

We'd passed our fair share of public comms in the commercial district, but we both knew the best access to public information would actually be in residential.

Cain stopped at a small cafe, tucked back out of the way of the majority of foot traffic, which was beginning to pick up, and we settled in at a table with an embedded comm panel.

"Order is a minimum of forty credits," a bored young human told us as she approached our table.

I expected some form of outraged protest from Cain, but he ordered and waved the woman off.

"Really?" I asked with a bit of skepticism.

"My actions are preventative. This way, I don't have to listen to you complain about being hungry later," he said.

I opened my mouth to say something in return but snapped it shut.

The waitress returned, and Cain, true to his word, told the woman everything was for me but a small cup of milk laced with picker-upper vanilla powder.

I sat there with my mouth hanging open as he picked up the steaming cup of milk.

"What?" he said. "I thought you don't like stims."

I didn't, but I hadn't expected him to remember that little detail.

I ate as he searched through the databases. On the whole, it was a letdown. Cain found out-of-date addresses and owner names for both companies, neither of which pinged the system. That, in and of itself, was a clue. No one escaped being registered or traced somehow within the system, not unless they were purposefully trying to hide. That was why the false identities we'd bought had cost so many credits—each of our presumed names had a realistic history of backlog activities to help scramble the real trace of digital fingerprints.

"What now?" I asked with a sigh. I leaned back into the padded crescent-shaped chair and pushed my stack of empty plates to one side.

"Now?" Cain said. "We wait."

Talk about boring. Hours of boring. Endless marching minutes of boring. Billions of nanoseconds of boring…

It was so boring, in fact, that I decided to do a refresher on the Opali-Poli region of the Lesser Seeds. It turned out to be where practitioners of the Lesser Seeds religion still traveled to, a mesmerizing and one-of-a-kind experience, according to the article. Having done their building at the time humans were still hunter-gatherers, the architects were a hotly contested topic with a wide range of proposed ideas that I won't bore you with.

But the Opali-Poli FloodGates of Knowledge was the main attraction, with a view to rival all views of the cosmos. It was built on the largest piece of one of the fractured moons—it and the subsequent debris formed fascinating rings around the Seed of Karth—which had a stable orbit due to little-understood technology. All cameras or image-capturing tech was outlawed for religious reasons, but the artwork it inspired was intriguing. Maybe I would add it to my list of places to see.

"A mesmerizing, unobstructed view of the Opali Yil nebula," read one caption under a particularly creative piece of art from the art enclaves on Yu. "Beautiful and rich colors abound, pulling the viewer into their warm embrace. No filters, just the naked eye staring into the tomb of Lo-Liopath-Poli. For all who follow the ardent of Poli, this is a must-see."

I delved a litter deeper into the religion and the history of the area. While it was a great little history lesson, I couldn't find any clues or possible leads that would help us unravel our little mystery. So I switched over to the news reports, mainly staying away from the news media as most had devolved into clickbait headlines with little to no actual information. But boredom forced me down unlikely rabbit holes, and thank goodness for that.

"Cain," I said. "Look."

He glanced over, scanned the headline, then shrugged.

I pouted, having expected a little more than that. I read the headline to him, "Protesters Upset over SeeClear Patch Debacle."

"That's your area of interest, not mine," he commented.

"Well, pull on your big boy pants and listen," I said.

He growled, and I grinned. *Now I'm getting somewhere.*

"Confore hands over SeeClear software updates to the developer, ignoring the plight of those outside heavily trafficked sections of space. Lunar 5 residents patiently waited for the patch to arrive, only to be turned away from the docking platform they'd been directed to. A new distribution center has been promised, but will Lunar 5 residents see it? Or will Confore let us down once again?" I sat back and let out a low whistle.

"It really was that easy," I commented when Cain didn't respond. "SeeClear and Project Clear Sight. Jorge had to be researching the 3.5 software patch."

"It would appear so," Cain finally said.

"That's it?"

He nodded and stood. *<It's time to go. We've waited long enough. We'll arrive there in time for me to do one last sweep.>*

"But what about the article? Now we can work to narrow down search parameters," I protested.

Cain turned and stared at me. *<Have you forgotten the countdown? Our focus must shift. We find the Star Eaters and deal with Miles's game. Then we can return to the issue of Jorge and Project Clear Sight.>*

He was right, and I blushed. I hadn't forgotten, but I'd let the Project Clear Sight mystery take center stage so that I wouldn't ruminate on all the things that might go wrong with the nanobots. It'd been a welcome distraction, but I hadn't stopped to consider if Cain had been able to push the matter away. The nanobots were floating around in his blood, after all.

As we left the cafe, Cain's mood darkened.

I peppered him with questions at first, wondering about contacting the IGJ or digging into their files. I thought I was helping, trying to take his mind off the Star Eaters and nanobot complications, but Cain snapped and said nothing else could be done through IGJ channels, that we would need clearance he didn't have in order to access any information about why the data had been purged.

I backed off and muttered my next inane suggestion more to myself than to Cain. "I wonder what Miles would have access to."

Cain whipped around and fixed me with a pair of solid emerald eyes and told me to drop it.

<All right, Mr. Grumpy.> I did. At least, I said no more out loud.

The only thing in the whole mess I was helpful with was the SeeClear hardware. The tech was chock-full of a bunch of goodies, full-spectrum vision enhancement, direct links to medical centers for detection of genetically inherited ocular maladies, tie-ins to holosimulations, and a host of other items. I'd read over the specs a dozen times, familiarizing myself with all the troubleshooting tips and back-channel ways to work out any bugs. But I couldn't think of anything that would necessitate an IGJ investigation, let alone get Jorge killed.

Even if a company was out there—and I was sure

there was—ripping off customers with knockoff hardware, no one cared. That was what the black market was for, and that was how a lot of new tech came into being. Crazy scientists without the constraints of governmental oversight were doing illicit engineering, free to do their mad-scientist scheming and invent for invention's sake.

I tried to shake off my frustration with not finding the lines connecting Jorge to the SeeClear tech. I was about to meet up with a bunch of Star Eaters—willingly.

We'd made it back to the Khepri neutral zone, and the engineered environment had cooled, imitating a pleasant summer's evening, with water sprinklers and drip lines activated. I wondered how many credits were needed to purchase the amount of water and specialized air scrubbers necessary to maintain such a beautifully manicured location.

Shallow pools lined with well-cut rock borders were host to a wide variety of aquatic Old Earth species, both animal and plant, and a few of the pools boasted extraterrestrial species as well. Fountains dotted the landscape, and the pleasing sounds of gently running water relaxed the casual observer. Flowering bushes, climbing vines, and artfully trimmed hedges created more than enough nooks and crannies for meetings. If not for the ever-present drones crossing the Khepri neutral zone in a grid pattern, it would've been a relaxing space to unwind.

Cain and I had still arrived early, not because of Miles's recommendation but so that Cain would have time to scout the area once more before the Star Eaters were scheduled to show up.

The food Cain had ordered for me turned into a hard lump in my gut as reality snuggled up really close to my brain.

Star Eaters. Again.

Maybe I should've been referring to them as the Celestial Light, but I didn't know if that mattered. There was the pesky issue of the message awaiting me at my lawyer's satellite office on Cleary Station. All I wanted was to get the meeting over with. It was the first step in getting through Miles's game and moving on to what really mattered.

"Offspring of Wats Hawking Orion has arrived," someone said from behind me.

I jumped and spun around. The pesky little buggers had been able to sneak up on me. I was beginning to suspect they always moved around in pairs. Those two were clothed in the same tightly woven blue robes as the ones from the *Rapscallion.*

"Have we met before?" *<They're here. Where are you?>*

"We have not traveled on this Ray."

<I'm here, behind you. Just keep talking. I'm watching.>

"I was told you would have further instructions for me. With this message business and all." I didn't want to waste time, not around those guys.

The Star Eaters turned toward each other, their robes rippling with the movement.

"Offspring of Wats Hawking Orion, you have been brought to us on a Ray of Deceit. We do not know of a message but only what must be bestowed upon you."

In sync, the Star Eaters lifted their arms—or whatever appendages functioned as arms, hidden beneath their voluminous robes—to pull back the edges of their hoods.

"What does that—" I started to ask then switched gears. "Wait, what are you—" I guessed they didn't have time for my questions.

From beneath their all-encompassing robes, a brilliant white light emerged. I was mesmerized by the light as it washed over me and embraced me in its warmth.

But as quickly as the light appeared, it vanished, and I felt abandoned by something I didn't understand. I staggered forward a few steps and cursed. I couldn't see anything but dark splotches when I blinked. Anxiety and uncertainty reared their ugly little heads, and I reached out, desperate for something to hold on to. A pair of hands grabbed my own and pulled me forward. I didn't need to ask—I knew those hands.

"What kind of waste-heap trick was that?" I asked as I continued blinking and tried to recover my vision. But the dark smudges wouldn't budge.

"They're gone."

"What did they do? I can't see." I tried not to flip into full-blown panic.

I'd been temporarily blinded by bright lights before, like when someone comes home from a long day at work, with the city in night mode, and without thinking, flips on the lights at full strength.

By the way, if you live in low-credit rentals, I don't recommend doing that. You'll see dermatex and a host of other unpleasant insects scramble back into their hidey-holes. It's much better to open the door, make some noise, then flip on the lights. Trust me on this.

"I don't know. I was far enough back it didn't affect me as it has you," Cain said. He released my hands, and his fingers brushed my face. He gently lifted each eyelid for a few seconds then tucked the stray wisps of hair behind my ears. "We should find a medical station."

I reached out, desperate for his hands. My fingers found his arms and sank into the soft cloth of his jacket. "What did you see?" When he didn't answer, I couldn't keep the panic out of my voice. "Cain? What do you see?"

One by one, his hands moved to take my own. "Your eyes are a little red and irritated."

"So, better safe than sorry?" I asked.

"Yes. Of course."

"Truth?" I asked. He was good at controlling our mental connection but not good enough to keep the edge of concern he exuded from touching my mind. I didn't need to see his face to know Cain hesitated in answering me.

"Your sclera is… completely red."

Temporary flash blindness shouldn't do that, not for the few seconds I was exposed.

My grip tightened on his hands. "Medical station it is."

Cain rearranged himself so that he led.

I realized, "There was no message. That little punk lied to me."

"I know."

"But how are we going to—"

"We'll deal with one issue at a time. Right now, we need to get your eyes checked out." The confidence in his voice was meant to be reassuring, but it was only slightly so.

"Should we contact Miles?" And by contact, I didn't mean to send a sweet little message to clarify things. I wanted the man to cough up answers about why he'd lied and what in Saturn's rings he was planning on doing to Cain.

"Better to leave that for a backup plan," Cain muttered.

With careful movements and murmured directions, Cain led me out of the Khepri neutral zone. If I hadn't been at war with my growing anxiety over both our situations, I would've been impressed that I ran into only one hedge.

I needed a lot of restraint to not let off some nervous quip about seeing-eye cats.

Vision or no vision, I knew when we crossed into the residential district. The air smelled different, even in the long-term residential district, where a fair sum of credits was undoubtedly handed over each month for the pleasure of living there. The greens held the smell of fresh air, of life and living, growing things. On any base, station, or ship, if they sported a hydroponics bay or green area such as a Khepri neutral zone, those spaces would hold the purest air. Upon moving away from them, the hint of recycled air with whiffs of metallic particles was a dead giveaway even in the richest areas.

Soon, Cain led me to a medical station. Basic bioscanner units were stocked with rudimentary first aid supplies. Moving to the stars had taught humanity harsh lessons. Medical and mechanical aid stations had grown in popularity soon after the construction of the first off-world base.

"Stand here," Cain said. His hand let go of me, and he touched my shoulders to turn me in the right direction. "I'm going to lift your arm and hold it up to the scanner," he said. "Now, turn around and hold still."

I'd used medical stations a few times before, after moving to the Original Luna base. The first time had felt like an extravagance. My father's work often had us camping long distances away from established bases or living areas, and he'd taught my brother and me how to pack and rely on ourselves for first aid needs.

This was why people who decide to go exploring in remote locations shouldn't skimp on the equipment. Believe me—the extra credits are worth it.

"The scan is complete. Hold on. It's printing orders," Cain told me.

The machine worked audibly with subtle whirrs and clicks as the paper wound, and the machine spat it out. An actual paper readout was a surprise. Paper is an expensive commodity. Either Lunar 5 was flush with credits, or we were standing in one of the richest districts I'd never laid eyes on.

"What does it say?" I asked, and my chest tightened at the possible news.

"Hold on," Cain mumbled.

"Cain," I growled, "what does it say?"

"It's an error report."

My stomach flip-flopped. "What in Saturn's rings does that mean?"

"Perhaps the HalfLife patch throws up the error

messages to ensure the privacy it's designed for," Cain answered with uncertainty behind his words.

"Do it again," I said.

His point was logical. The patches were designed to protect our privacy. I hadn't considered that little hiccup but wanted to make sure.

I let Cain take me through the process again.

"Well?"

"Error report."

"Dammit."

All right. Not a lot of great options. A medical facility carried its own set of risks. I was sure some doctors were used to being bribed about keeping things secret, but a good oath-sworn doc might feel it necessary to report my true bioinfo if they deemed my condition serious enough. Or we could run into a do-good doc who might feel it necessary to do the area a favor and turn us in.

Plus, we didn't have the intimidation of Miles High standing with us to make sure the bribes went through without a hitch.

Being logged into the system wouldn't be the worst thing that could happen, though.

<No.>

"Those were private musings." I reached out to poke him in the chest but missed. "Now I'm annoyed." I kept reaching out until I realized the crafty bugger was dodging me. "Stand still."

"If we get logged into the system, how do you think we're going to get past their checkpoints on our way out?"

"Maybe I'll settle down and make Lunar 5 my new home?" I teased but quickly sobered. "Besides, maybe they can help remove your bots. Or deactivate them."

"Doubtful."

I sighed. "So now what, oh wise agent of the IGJ?" Picturing the scowl on his face, I grinned despite the seriousness of the situation.

"We go back to the Rio Latte. Give your eyes a chance to recoup. Go from there."

I wasn't enamored with his plan for one big, annoying reason. "So we wait for you to explode? Is that the plan?"

"As I've stated on multiple occasions, Miles likes his games. I've no doubt the countdown is genuine. He likes to make people uncomfortable," Cain said. "We have three days, fifteen and a half hours before our week is up. By Old Earth standards. Time enough to figure out what Miles is actually angling for."

"I'm impressed. Except for one thing. Lunar 5 doesn't have the same length of days as Old Earth. Their day is thirty-three hours long. Which technically gives us more time," I corrected him.

"Wrong. Miles always goes by the length of days on Old Earth. Either he can't shake the habit, or he enjoys messing with people. I'll let you guess which one it is," Cain said sourly.

"Fine. Three days, fifteen and a half hours left. But it's not much time."

"Time enough for you to rest." *<I will not take no for an answer,>* Cain added.

My instinct to resist was there, but my growing concern over my eyes overrode any witty comebacks I might have crafted. I held out my arm in defeat, and Cain led me back to the Rio Latte.

The change in air additives alerted me the moment we entered the hotel's lobby. Rio Latte air held the hint of lavender with the musky perfume famous on Gali Prime. Cain helped me move through the lobby and over to the lifts.

"Excuse me, may we have a moment of your time?" someone asked.

<Advert bot?> I mentally asked Cain.

He didn't respond to me, only to whoever or whatever had done the talking. "We could do with some peace and quiet. Perhaps this could wait until the morning?"

"You've been selected for a free promotional tour of the best Lunar 5 has to offer. If you'd wait here in the lobby—"

I spoke up. "We're not interested."

"Then perhaps I can interest you in free tickets to the Lunar Heritage Museum. It's a fabulous way to spend the afternoon. If you would head over to the reception desk, they can print out the tickets."

"I said we're not interested," Cain growled. *<Advert bots need to be banned.>*

<Surely, you jest. They're just doing their jobs. Can't hang around for a few more minutes to satisfy the thing, huh?>

<If it doesn't leave, I permanently disable it.>

"How about a free meal at the Oat Tab? The front desk can provide a voucher if you wait—"

"Customer satisfaction code three eight nine two seven," a male interrupted. "Sorry about that. Corporate sponsors and all."

Cain shifted our weight, and I tried to smile, hoping I didn't look like a total buffoon.

"Is everything all right, ma'am?"

"Yes, thank you," Cain replied. "She's tired and had a few too many celebratory drinks. We're heading up for the evening."

"Ma'am?"

<Look to your left and giggle,> Cain ordered.

<Yes, sir.>

I swung my head to the left then dropped my eyes to what I presumed was the floor. Everything was still a bright glowing mess for me. "Engaged," I said with enough giggles to mask the real giggle of uncertainty. The word had just slipped out. I have no idea where it came from, honest.

"Congratulations! Please wait a moment," the man said.

"Thank you, but no. We need to head to our room and get some rest," Cain said.

"Sir, it's our pleasure to celebrate with you and this lovely young lady," the man replied.

I heard one click then another.

"I said no. Thank you," Cain snapped. "We don't need vintage memorabilia."

"It's complimentary and will only take a moment to process—"

"No," Cain growled, and his fingers dug into my side as he pushed me forward.

I wished I could have seen the expression on the man's face, and I wondered exactly what color Cain's eyes were.

<None of your business.>

<Quit being a spoilsport. What did the man want, anyway?>

I'm not sure Cain's intrusion on my thoughts bothered me as much as the notion had only a few weeks ago.

<Pictures.>

The lift must have arrived, because Cain suddenly pulled me along with him, and I felt a whoosh of air and the floor giving way.

As soon as we were upstairs in the room, I shed my jumpsuit, and when I was ready, Cain helped me lie down.

When he was finished, he reached out and squeezed my hands. As he was ready to let go, I tightened my grip, but Cain gently unwound my fingers from his.

<I'm right here. I'm not going anywhere.>

Famous last words.

14

Nightmares

Before I awoke to a nightmare, I dreamed, but not of the *Rapscallion*, Mrs. Gol, or believe it or not, Cain.

The dream was of the time I'd spent on Epo-5, a miserable little backwater of a planet coated in waste bogs and long-forgotten ruins that my father believed held some great galactic secret. I was seven when he was assigned to reexamine a set of ruins featured in a number of conflicting academic papers produced by students assigned to the planet a few years prior.

No one could've been better to work out the conflicting data than Wats Hawking Orion.

Speculation ran rampant over which species had built the once-sprawling cities on Epo-5. One popular theory discussed the possibility of a species that had risen to a cultural level equivalent to the major indigenous populations on what had once been North and South America on Old Earth.

For nonhistory buffs, those were continents before World War IV destroyed most of them. The more familiar name was the Palo Verde Waste Lands.

Anyway, a few popular theories were floating around in academic circles. Either the inhabitants of Epo-5 were decimated by their own kind or their own hubris or by neighboring feuds or some such warfare, or an extraterrestrial species wiped them out. Extraterrestrials were the dominant theory, supported by the debris patterns—lack of debris in some cases—and craters, where higher-density populations were believed to have been.

Why another species would travel to the system, target the Epo-5 culture, and wipe them out when Epo-5 hadn't even hit an industrial phase puzzled those who believed in some different answer.

That wasn't knowledge I walked around spouting as a seven-year-old. I was a bright kid but not that interested in theoretical debates. I only became interested in it all after my father's arrest. I'd thought digging into everything he'd done might provide some answers. Because he'd kept copious notes, once the IGJ returned them, I spent most of my research hours on Epo-5 looking at every report or rumor my father had collected on the planet.

He'd been looking for something.

I cannot tell you what that was—never could figure it out.

Only that Po—my father, whatever, the man who was Wats Hawking Orion—was fascinated by what was left of the intricate maze of above- and belowground cities peppered throughout the planet.

Underground research was a no go, at least in the flesh, thanks to the neighboring Sici, who had used the planet as a dump for their waste fuel before upgrading to a more ecologically friendly energy system.

But with the proper inoculations and precautions, exploration and work were possible topside.

Exterior walls that still stood revealed a species or at least a segment of the species who valued precision, symmetry, and functional art. Three different sizes of stones had been used in recurring patterns as the species built their aboveground cities. Beautiful geometrical designs would float above me as my brother and I played and our father worked.

Compact air recyclers with the main unit housed in our ground suits, its tubing hooked onto our nostrils, kept away the worst of the waste-bog stench. I don't think I'll ever forget how my brother and I dared each other to see who could unhook from our air units the longest.

You should have seen the look on my father's face when he found out what we were doing. We didn't know the air recyclers also worked at keeping the worst of the toxins out of our systems. But we didn't stop. My record was two minutes and thirty-seven seconds. My brother never beat me.

When I awoke in the little room in Rio Latte, it was to the memory of the stench of Epo-5 and the geometrical patterns floating above me.

I cautiously opened one eyelid then, with delight, popped the other open. The black blobs of doom were gone. *Leave it to my cranky* IGJ *man to know what to do.*

A huge grin split my face. The saying is cliché: you never know what you have until you lose it, and I'm not making light of anyone's situation. But after being temporarily blinded for a few hours, having my vision restored felt like a miracle.

I sat up, pushed back the covers, and was ready to gush about my good news when I turned, and my eyes fell on the chair.

Cain was gone.

Absolute, one-hundred-percent, pure-grade irrational panic seized my heart and mind. I couldn't breathe, and I would've sworn the room spun.

Cain's jacket wasn't draped over the back of the chair. My eyes swung toward the small bathroom. The lights were off. No one was in the room except me.

Stop playing the fool. When did you become so irrational?

"Cain?" I said, unable to help myself, then followed up with <Where are you?>

I waited. I whispered. I asked.

Nothing but an eerie silence settled over the room. I untangled my legs from the rest of the covers, got up, then moved about the room like a ship without a guidance system. My actions were driven by some type of need I couldn't verbalize. I looked in every nook and cranny for some kind of hint. But I found no note, no whisper of a clue.

Unable to sit and wait, I left the room and hurried down the hall. As I approached the lift, I felt a heaviness in my mind, an irrational feeling of anxiety and panic I'd never experienced before, not even after the IGJ hauled me into one of their centers for questioning. A small, still rational part of my mind wanted to know why in the worlds I would act this way over some guy. *Have I snapped mentally? Did the Star Eaters do something with that whole sketchy light show?*

If someone had cornered me and demanded to know what was going on, I would've been a blubbering fool. All I knew was that Cain had vanished with no warning, no note, and no reasonable explanation as to why.

By the time the lift reached the main floor, I was ready to crawl out of my skin. I shoved my way past two Telt tourists, impervious to their raised ruffs of razor-sharp fur at my impropriety. I marched up to the front desk and pounded on the counter.

The poor man who'd tried to offer us the celebratory drink in honor of our "engagement" popped up. His pale face grew white, and his wide-eyed expression did nothing but ramp up my panic.

He raised his hands. "Please. We're required to comply with all authorities. I have no—"

"Where is he? Did he leave a note? Do you know where he is?" The questions tumbled out. "I woke up, and he's not in our room. Just gone, with no message or anything."

"Ma'am, please," the man insisted. "Calm down. I'm sure everything will be resolved, and your fiancé will be back soon."

"How do you know that? How?"

Beads of sweat appeared on his brow. "Your fiancé left the Rio Latte less than thirty minutes ago. I'm sure he'll be back as soon as he can."

I gripped the edge of the counter, my head swimming with emotions. That small rational voice tried to make itself heard above my emotional nonsense. *Good grief,*

Mahia, get a grip. Cain had probably gone to get breakfast, just like the day before.

The man tried again in a more dignified tone. "Please, I'm sure he'll return soon."

I trembled, staring at the man, trying to force myself to see reason. Cain would come back. He would. As I repeated those words silently, over and over, that small rational voice pushed itself between the panic and anxiety. I closed my eyes and pictured Cain stepping into our room with another platter of something delicious in his hands. *That's right, stay focused.*

When I popped my eyes open, the man had moved to help the offended Telts but was still nervously eyeing me. I backed away from the desk, forced myself to smile—trying to look appeased and not insane—then spun around and headed back to the lifts.

When I reached my floor, a wave of embarrassment washed over me. *You're such a fool. What were you thinking?*

I forced myself to take deep, even breaths as I walked down the hallway and stepped into the room, letting the rational part of my mind consider why in Saturn's rings I'd had such a drastic reaction to Cain's absence. I wasn't some helpless girl who had to have a man take care of her. I'd carved a life for myself out of unbearable circumstances, and this wasn't even a tenth of what I'd gone through before.

As I closed the door behind myself, scanning the room once more, I felt an intense realization that something wasn't right. I took my time and moved about the room. Everything seemed to be in place—nothing out of the ordinary.

I sat down on the edge of the bed and waited. And the realization hit me.

I had several questions I'd never asked regarding our ability to communicate telepathically. I chalked up my lack of curiosity to an overload of information, and the telepathic communication had been a pleasant surprise overall. Without it, we might not have survived.

The one concrete aspect about the whole situation was the faint buzzing sensation at the base of my skull, signaling Cain's presence. Even when he'd distanced himself on the *Whimsy*, I'd known he was still there, just silent and sulking.

But suddenly, his presence was completely gone. Nothing was there but the empty silence of my own thoughts. The realization pressed down on me, freezing me in place. My fingers dug into the sheets to grab something tangible, and my eyes wouldn't leave the chair Cain had slept in.

The dump of adrenaline and anxiety had tied my stomach up in knots—those stupid things were threatening to take up permanent residence, and I should've started charging rent—and as it unwound itself, I got up and raced to the bathroom.

Eventually, everything settled, and as I had found the answer to my irrational reaction, I grew annoyed. *Blast that insufferable man out of an air lock.* He could've told me, warned me. And I kicked myself for not asking questions, a lot more questions.

I still felt a lingering haze of anxiety but was mostly myself once again—as long as I stayed focused. I glanced at the Sur-T Screen's date and was relieved to confirm it was indeed just the day after the ill-fated meeting with the Star Eaters.

That led me to only one thought: *Miles*. The sneaky piece of garbage had betrayed me, set me up with the Star Eaters for Pluto only knows why, and had toyed with Cain for his own malicious pleasure. Maybe he'd realized we were onto him and gone ahead and done something to Cain. *But why? What in the worlds could be his motivation?*

Both men had made their dislike of the other as obvious as a reactor's afterglow. Cain frequently referred to our situation as one of Miles's games. Nothing would've kept Miles from getting bored and deciding to throw the switch on Cain's nanobots.

Cain had frequently said Miles enjoyed his games. Perhaps I'd been just a lure to create some horrible death scenario for Cain, and that was why I couldn't feel his telepathic presence anymore, because Miles had flipped a switch.

As I sat there, my certainty grew that Miles was behind Cain's abrupt disappearance, and with each passing second, my hatred for Miles grew.

When the hate burned away the last of my brain fog, I felt disgusted with myself. I didn't really know much about Cain, other than some mysterious connection that had been thrust upon us without me being asked. I'd let myself grow very attached to the man, and quickly too. And I was acting like a baby because he was gone. I'd been left before, and this situation wasn't any different.

But I knew what it actually was—I just couldn't face the reason right at that moment. I pushed those thoughts away and concentrated on what I could turn my attention to.

If I reported Cain's absence, the authorities would be called. In fact, I realized I should make nice with the man at the lobby desk, or he might get an itch to call the authorities himself. Lunar 5 might not play well with the IGJ, but that didn't mean they'd ignore serious accusations of someone going missing. That kinds of rumor was bad for business.

In the calm before the storm, I stood and pulled on my jumpsuit. Once dressed, I splashed cold water on my face, redid my braid, and left the room.

I went downstairs, apologized, and told the nervous man how I'd had a pretty bad nightmare on top of a killer hangover, and I'd missed the message Cain had sent to meet up at one of the cafes. I made a few jokes about what a total nutcase I was, and the poor man simply nodded. I'm not sure if he believed me, but I couldn't do much else.

Next up. Find Miles.

The man had told us where he was staying, so I just needed to go there and make him talk. As I settled into the idea, I realized it was the logical solution. By the time I left Rio Latte, I was positive I would find Miles and force the man to answer for what he'd done. Because if Miles wasn't going to play nice, then neither was I.

The universe had taken everything from me: my pops, my brother, my home, my job. But it had at least seen fit to make up some difference with Cain. But just as I was trying to learn to trust, to open up, to be okay with relying on another for help, the universe realized its error and said, "Nope. Whoops. Forgot. Mahia Orion can't have any of the nice toys."

I didn't talk about it much, not even to myself, but a void existed inside me. I'd tried to fill it by focusing on keeping my nose clean and being a good employee. Those were flimsy med patches when a full-on level-ten wound-care treatment kit was needed.

Cain had begun to be that, as silly as that might sound.

And for the first time in a long time, I felt the gnawing presence of that void, already eating at the parts of me Cain had begun to heal. And as the void returned, deeper and darker, I knew it would threaten to turn me into something I didn't recognize.

The worlds hated my father for his betrayal of humanity. Now I was learning how others also hated my brother. *Why not add my name to the Let's Hate the Orion Family List?*

Little else mattered, only the certainty that Miles would pay for what he'd done.

15

Raging against the Madman

I did take one other precaution, though. When I stopped at the front desk, I dumped a load of credits for an upgrade on the room, a two-day privacy package. I giggled and blushed about the engagement and resulting innuendos.

The upgrade came with a wide variety of local businesses the customer was able to choose from, to deliver anything someone could imagine. By the time the system cycled through all the additional questions, I was ready to punch the screen.

If the front desk decided my erratic behavior warranted a follow-up, at least a bunch of sticky red tape would be there to wade through in order to lift the privacy upgrade.

The program processed my refusals, and a holoimage of an annoyingly chipper young man appeared beside the front desk.

"We've recognized you as a preferred customer. Are you sure you don't wish to take advantage of the local offers?"

"I'm sure," I replied.

"We thank you for choosing our services to suit your needs. Have a pleasant—"

"I do have one request," I realized. "What is the fastest route to the Emerald Oasis?"

"Head west on Periphery then turn right to head north on Alabaster. The Emerald Oasis is one of the newer establishments in this district. Founded in—"

I turned and walked off. The history of the hotel wasn't relevant.

With each step down Periphery, I pictured how everything would play out. Miles would be expecting me, no doubt. If I didn't come to him, I was sure he was planning on coming to me. He'd set up the whole endeavor of getting me to meet those Star Eaters, and I had no doubt he needed to get some angle out of the whole twisted plan. Even though everything would play out on his turf, at least I would have the advantage of surprise.

I would find Miles, and he would grant me access and lead me to his room, where he and his hired thugs would be waiting. No doubt, security at the Oasis would do a sweep and confiscate the Vulture.

That wouldn't be an issue.

My plan, born out of an ill-conceived haze, was to get close enough to snatch his cane and use his own weapon against him.

I turned north on Alabaster and spotted the gaudy hotel front only a few meters ahead. Shoulders back, I marched up to the front doors, located beneath a glaring neon sign. The sensor was triggered, and they slid open.

But before I had a chance to assess the layout of the lobby, Miles ran right into me. He hissed as he regained his footing and shot out of the hotel lobby.

My body moved before my brain caught up with what was going on. I spun and ran after him. We raced along Alabaster, and when Miles swung left to slip between two more buildings, I did the same.

By the time we were through the narrow alley and moving down another street, my brain was up to date with current events.

"Miles High!" I called out. "You're going to tell me the truth about the Star Eaters, then you're going to pay for what you've done to Cain."

The man spared a moment to glance over his shoulder, but that was all. We raced through the residential district and into the commercial.

My ego crowed with delight. Miles High was afraid of me. He'd known I was coming, and out of time, he'd scuttled off in fear.

Miles darted to the right and ducked into what I presumed was a warehouse. Not hesitating, I followed. A dimly lit hallway greeted me as I stepped inside. Miles stood off to one side, hands on his knees while he wheezed.

"I'm sorely lacking on my cardio." He coughed.

I marched up to him and pushed, and Miles tumbled to the ground. With a snarl, I stomped my foot down on his neck, hard. He looked completely shocked as his mouth opened, and he gurgled in pain.

Delight coursed through me, and I bent forward. "Just another part of your game?"

That was where my ego-fueled idiocy stopped.

He lifted his legs and gave me a good, swift kick. He might not have been up with his cardio workouts, but he was a limber sucker. The kick sent me stumbling forward, and before I could turn and balance myself, Miles was up and had landed a firm punch on the right side of my lower back.

"Where's Cain? What did you do to him?" I snarled, ignoring the pain.

"What are you going on about? I haven't done anything to the vermin." Miles's voice was calm and even. I was expecting a hint of crazy crime-boss indignation in there, or annoyed madman.

"You're a lousy liar. You've done something. I met with the Star Eaters, and there was no message. You just made up some kind of excuse to toy with him, didn't you?" I spat.

"You daft idiot. Do you really think this is all about him?"

"You hated him. He hated you."

"Of course. But I had to nudge you in the right direction."

"The right direction? You think the Star Eaters are the right direction my life should be taking about now?"

Before Miles had a chance to say anything, the lights in the base abruptly went out. The city had flipped to night mode in the middle of the day. As a voice thundered across the base, orange hazard lights flickered on outside.

"Attention, inhabitants of Lunar 5. We apologize for this interruption in your daily schedule. It has come to our attention there are two fugitives who need immediate capture. Your assistance is required. If you have any information regarding the whereabouts of Mahia Eimariana Orion, also known as Kimmi Washlo, and Zhu Akio, also known as Miles High, also known as Darren Lighthouse, please contact the InterGalactic Justice agent nearest you."

I stared at Miles. "Darren?"

"It was a last-minute deal that went sideways, but the alias stuck." He shrugged.

"What in Jupiter's name is going on?" I asked.

He replied with a line from a standard jute-store story. "Come with me if you want to find out."

Talk about your charmer. Cue eye rolls.

"Tell me what's going on," I insisted instead. "What did you do to Cain? Why the Star Eaters?"

Miles straightened and stared at me. "I haven't done anything to Cain… yet. But right now, it would seem our little party is about to be crashed. I knew I should've just purged the whole crew of the *Whimsy*, not just the captain and those goons. How many credits does it take to buy loyalty anymore?"

"Are you trying to tell me the IGJ was the higher bidder?"

That was absurd, but I decided I would play along for the time being.

"We need to get out of here. You can ask your questions when we're secure." Not waiting for me to protest, Miles simply moved past me and walked down the hallway. He stopped in front of a door and tapped his foot on the floor as he stared at it. Maybe he was admiring its standard precut frame or contemplating the door's existence in a sea of hundreds of thousands of look-alikes.

I knew I could've cut my losses and taken off. I could've tried to dodge the IGJ until they caught me then pleaded with them to listen to my story and throw more credits at my lawyers to get me out of the jam.

But I wanted to know what had happened to Cain. I had no doubt Miles wasn't above lying to me. He could've activated Cain's nanobots and was skirting around the issue. Then again, I wasn't ready to rule out the IGJ, but I had no idea why they would take him and leave me behind.

Oh, curse the planets. I'd been the bait for Miles. That was why I was still there and Cain wasn't. I connected the dots. Someone on the *Whimsy* must've tipped off the IGJ. Then the old-fashioned photograph from the nervous man behind the counter verified our identities, and asking directions to the Emerald Oasis had been the cherry on top for the IGJ to swoop in. *Fudge nuggets and a whole shipload of other words.*

But why in the worlds did they assume I would run to him, of all people?

"So, what's up with the door?" I asked as I moved to stand next to him.

"Nothing. Just waiting for you to make up your mind." He shrugged. "Place your palm on the door."

"And why would I do that?"

"Just do what I do and hold still." Miles reached out and flattened his palm against the door. But the hairs on his arms were what held my interest as they stood up.

Well, fudge.

I slammed my hand against the door and held still. My skin tingled as a bolt of electricity ran through the door then through my body. A part of me was fascinated by what was about to happen, while another part of me was absolutely terrified.

16

Déjà vu

Teleportation, or its more common name, "zap 'n' roll," had been the hot new item a few centuries back. Odds are, if you're reading this, that your grandparents or great-grandparents were among the lucky ones who never tried out the system.

You probably studied it in school as one of those we're-grateful-for-technology-but be-careful-what-you-wish-for campaigns. Even with my nontraditional education, I studied the decade referred to as the Great Undoing.

Being able to travel instantaneously from one location to another was the dream that haunted humanity. When the difficulties appeared to have been worked out, the governments rolled out the red carpet, and tech stock soared until five years later, when everything fell apart.

That was quite literal for the people who had been frequent users of teleportation tech. Once reports rolled in, covering the molecular damage that occurred due to repeated use of any type of teleportation technology, scientists and engineers scrambled to figure out the issues and keep their jobs. But as public sentiment turned against the tech, with no viable fix in sight, the idea was scratched.

Presently, engineering schools and tech giants steer clear of the tech—not just human-based companies either.

Popular theory believes the Kei were the closest to perfecting the technology. A vid of one of their scientists pops up now and again, with a rumored fifty or more teleport times logged, before his molecular structure fell apart. Don't ever watch that. Please, trust me on this.

A less popular theory, but one which never surprised me, was that the Eeri mastered the tech. If that was true, they didn't share.

Another group of rumors about a famous heavy metal rock band, Flaming Fuel, discusses how the group hid secret messages in their lyrics, stating that the Old Earth monarchy had perfected the tech but kept it secret for their own personal use.

I guess the heavy rockers were right. Go figure.

After the flash of electricity ran through me, I opened my eyes to find I wasn't in Kansas anymore—Old Earth movie reference. If you haven't seen it, you should check it out.

Instead of the warehouse hallway, I was standing in the middle of a rather large command deck. I might or might not have patted myself down to make sure I was all there.

Miles gave me an amused smirk before turning to

face a rather sharply dressed woman standing on the captain's dais. I knew that command deck, that layout.

"What the hell? Why am I on the *Rapscallion*?" I asked.

Everyone ignored me.

"Report," Miles said.

"Sir. The IGJ has locked down Lunar 5. Our operatives are reporting widespread searches being conducted. But still no word on the IGJ agent, Turen ed-Suren, sir."

With my mouth unceremoniously hanging open, I stared at Miles. Questions were piling up on each other like an unruly nest of little Glipglows, but I found myself at a loss for words.

"Contrary to the persona I provide the public, I am neither mad nor in charge of a criminal organization," Miles stated calmly. "Well, that's not entirely true. The Little Asteroids do work for me, but Julian Compti is the top-level bad guy"—he turned away but then threw me a wink—"and I may or may not be mad. My psychiatrists and medical personnel argue over the finer points of my lucidity."

"The *Rapscallion*?" I squeaked as a few images of a deranged Mrs. Gol abruptly popped into my head.

"Ah. Yes. Why don't we find a place that's a little more comfortable and get a bite to eat while we talk."

"Stunned" wouldn't even begin to describe how I felt. With wide eyes, I looked around the command deck. The officers, or whatever their designation might've been, were more than just human, and all wore black pants and jackets with crisp yellow shirts underneath. A few individuals bore one or more silver stripes down their jackets' left arms, while the captain had two additional stripes on her right. It was a style of uniform I wasn't familiar with.

With my jaw scraping the floor, I followed Miles in a fog. The layout was identical to the *Rapscallion*, and I shivered as a ghostly image of Cain moved past me. Miles took me to one of the command deck's offices. But instead of being dark and abandoned, the office was equipped with plush seating that lined the walls, three oversized Sur-T Screens, and… a pool—I kid you not. A literal pool sat in the middle of the room, stocked with koi and freshwater lilies.

Miles caught me gaping. "An automatic force field engages if there are any alerts or unexpected maneuvers. If prolonged combat is called for, a stabilizing agent is added to the water, effectively putting the fish and plants in a form of suspended animation."

"Why?" It was the one question that seemed to encompass everything.

Miles laughed, a full-on belly laugh, and turned toward a communications node. The man ordered more food than the two of us could eat in a week.

When finished, he shrugged. "Old habits. Please, sit."

I took a few steps back and collapsed into one of the chairs. My brain was on overload.

"First, we're not on board the *Rapscallion*. We're on the *Samaritan*, a twin to the *Rapscallion*," Miles said.

After my brain caught up, I said, "I was under the impression schematics for ships similar to the *Rapscallion* had been scrapped."

Miles nodded. "They were. But do you really think

we built only one from that design? It was just a front for the public, the ship we paraded about while the rest did the real work, the stuff we weren't keen on having the media get wind of."

"How many?"

"Four. The *Jester* and the *Crown* were destroyed in battle."

"Seriously? Who was in charge of naming them?"

Miles's lighthearted gaze fell into a wounded expression.

"Oh no. Uh-uh. Please tell me it wasn't you," I said.

The man pulled out a handkerchief with a flourish and held it up against his mouth. With an offended air, he said, "My sister did. She was eight at the time. Our popo was indulgent with her."

I slumped into the overly soft cushion of my chair and determined I had to be dreaming. Everything from Cain missing to Miles whisking me away to some private fleet was a nightmare, a twisted jute-store novel my mind had concocted in order to make sense of what was going on—not to mention the fact that we were entirely off course from our original purpose, resolving the mystery of Project Clear Sight. I needed a moment to regroup.

Lost in my thoughts, I didn't realize Miles had stood and moved over to where I was sitting in a daze. He leaned over and snapped his fingers.

"We haven't even begun to slip into the black hole of oblivion. You're going to need to do better than this, Ms. Orion." He straightened as I focused on him. "If you want to see this through, of course."

"See this through?"

Miles tilted his head to the side and frowned. "I had expected better, but I suppose some allowances must be made."

I didn't know if I was more offended by his word choice or his tone. Either way, I shot up and punched him. "Allowances?" I fumed. "If you're telling me you're not a dream or some break of sanity, then you'd better start giving me answers, or else there's going to be another crime scene to investigate."

Miles moved his jaw back and forth. "Good. I'm glad to see you're still in there."

"Enough with the riddles. Do you nefarious-type figures go to riddle school or something? Is it a requirement for you guys? Some kind of club?"

"But isn't that what your father prepared you for?"

Though Miles didn't physically touch me, I felt as if he'd hit me in the gut. "No. My father didn't prepare me for anything, considering he up and abandoned me." I took a deep breath to steady myself. "Either you tell me what's going on, or…" I tapped my bracelet. The Vulture unfolded, the weapon encased my arm, and with a calm, steady movement, I raised my arm. "Or I will shoot."

"Go ahead," Miles said as if he didn't have a care in the world.

I fired.

I should have thought it through. First, I was standing too close to the target. If the weapon had fired, I would have been covered in, well, debris. Second, I should've known the Vulture wouldn't work. No doubt, some variation of dampening field was in play to prevent it from working.

"Interesting choice," Miles mused as he moved back to his seat. "If you're truly serious about finding answers to your questions."

With the loss of control over what was happening to me and the rage building inside, I scanned the room for anything useful as a weapon, something to force Miles into providing the answers I wanted instead of more riddles.

The only item in the room I could get my hands on was an Old Earth vase serving as a flowerpot for a plant that had several beautiful yellow blooms. It was delicately perching on a pedestal, framed by three lights. If I couldn't use it as a weapon, I could at least do some damage.

I whirled around and leaped to the delicate blue-and-white porcelain piece. When it wouldn't budge, I took aim with the Vulture. I looked at Miles and caught a little twitch at the corner of his mouth. *Good.*

The light, teasing note in his voice was gone, but Miles gestured toward where I'd been sitting. "Please. Our food will be here shortly."

"Answers, not more food."

The door slid open and revealed two heavily armed soldiers.

"Ms. Orion, we can make this experience quite unpleasant, even painful, if that's what you wish. Or you can take a seat, and we'll talk." Miles took a breath and added, "Of course, I do relish a good old-fashioned interrogation session."

I was trapped in more ways than one and wondered when my life had become so complicated.

Right, when I was born to a man like Wats Hawking Orion. If only time travel existed.

As angry as I was, interrogation didn't sound appealing. "Fine. You win." I deactivated the Vulture and mustered my best help desk smile. "Happy?"

I sat down, knowing I'd been fooling myself all along. I didn't have a good hand—heck, I didn't even have any cards to play. Getting off the ship without his permission wasn't going to be possible, and Jupiter only knew where the ship was currently located. We could still have been orbiting Lunar 5 or on our way to who-knew-where.

"Not quite. I am rather hungry," Miles answered.

"Then get a food dispenser."

"They never seem to get the taste quite right, do they?" Miles leaned back. "But while we wait, I'll try to answer some of your questions."

17

A Girl's Got to Eat

"Let's start with the most pressing, the matter of your heart's blood—our infamous IGJ agent, Turen ed-Suren, better known as Cain," Miles said with a flourish.

I do believe he expected me to clap with glee at his theatrical statement.

With an obvious pout, he continued. "As I'm sure you heard our good captain say, there haven't been any updates on the man. Not that I'm complaining. Cain has been a thorn in my side for too long. But for your sake"—he leaned toward me—"I'll switch sides and vote for him still being alive."

I crossed my arms and scowled.

"I do have a few theories as to what happened. Care to hear them?"

"No. Just spit it out. Did you or did you not detonate the nanobots?"

Miles took in a deep breath then slowly exhaled. "No. I didn't. And we're still well within the time frame I programmed into my little helpers. Now, as to my theories."

One tiny, little knot in my stomach unwound itself. So he was alive for the time being.

"There are factions within factions within factions of every government, company, and societal structure, something I'm sure is not a revelation to you. But under normal circumstances, most factions tend to work alongside the others for the greater good of whatever that may be—governments ruling over their constituents, company bonuses in order to add value to keep employees... Well, you understand.

"The IGJ is one of those agencies, which houses multiple factions with different beliefs on how to police such a vast amount of space, not to mention dealing with a myriad of cultural and societal expectations."

I tried not to show interest but sat up a little straighter.

"Wats Hawking Orion sparked outrage across the known worlds. But he also sparked something else, curiosity. And that curiosity led to many dark places the majority of seekers couldn't stomach, but for the few that could, questions and doubts were raised.

"You and Cain, whether by accident or design, have stumbled into one of these dark, nebulous crevices where too many are still trying to put together the pieces of the puzzle. And now, he has become one of those pieces. But which faction has taken it upon themselves to host such an elaborate misdirect? I don't know. And it's far too dangerous to speculate. Allegiances are shifting much too often for my taste."

I decided to break my silence. "So, what all of that gobbledygook you just spewed boils down to is that someone or a group of someones within the IGJ took Cain."

"If that is all you can hear, then for now, yes."

When Miles took a breath, ready to continue pontificating, the door opened, and the food was delivered. I contemplated not eating, knowing that would annoy Miles.

The two men who brought the food laid it out with flourish on the table. Pristine white napkins wiped the edges of crystal dishes, and each man made slight adjustments to the orientation and position of each plate until they were satisfied.

With Miles's connections and the memory of the quality of food his chef had prepared on Epsilon's Station, I knew what I saw here would be several times better.

A tray of braised megolo sat in front of me, steam wafting up from the tender pink strips of meat garnished with green and yellow herb sauces. Next to it sat a plate of Neetho-raised poli-fish, their unique blue flesh coated in melting pats of butter.

Tucked around the meat were plates piled high with a wide variety of vegetables. I recognized a few from Old Earth, but the majority were ones I had no knowledge of. I did spy a bowl of genie beans, genetically enhanced black beans that were a staple for all colonists. They were easy to grow and hardy and could be stored for months. From the looks of those genie beans, I guessed they'd been cooked in a heavy trumtra sauce.

Decision made, I loaded up my plate.

"How do we get Cain back?" I asked around a mouth-ful of watersnips marinated in garlic and ginger and tossed with sesame seeds.

Did you know that a single vial of sesame seeds went for over five hundred credits on the black market? I felt like I was eating pure gold.

"I've got personnel on the ground and a few IGJ agents on retainer. When they find something, they'll report in," Miles answered.

"That's great, but how are *we* going to find Cain?"

Miles looked up and grinned. "Eat, then we'll see."

I didn't want to wait, but the food lulled me into a heavy state of complacency, at least physically. It didn't dampen my questions, though.

"What about the Star Eaters? Why did you lie about the message?" I waved my arm at him for good measure. "All they did was flash a bright light, which blinded me for a bit."

The question caught him off guard. He'd praised my smarts often enough, so he surely would've realized I wouldn't forget about that little hitch in his grand scheme.

Miles took a bite of his megolo, chewed, and dabbed at his mouth. "A necessary misdirect."

"Misdirect?" I paused with a forkful of poli-fish halfway to my mouth. "That's all you have to say?"

My fingers tightened around the handle of the fork, and my other hand moved to grip the knife.

"The Star Eaters were to offer you... a few options."

"Options? And what, pray tell, were those oh-so-fab-ulous options supposed to be?" I asked.

"I can explain it, or I can show you. Which do you prefer?"

"Show me."

Miles nodded. "Then finish your food, and we'll take a deep dive into the mysterious world of the Celestial Plain."

I speared my last piece of poli-fish, and the awareness of Cain's absence washed over me unexpectedly. I'd grown accustomed to his presence and desperately wanted to hear his stoic, unhelpful comments whispered from his mind to mine.

More than that, no matter what happened, how chaotic or unpredictable things might get, Cain would've been there for me. The man had become a port in my storm, a quiet strength I hadn't realized I'd needed until he was gone.

"Out of mild curiosity," Miles said, "has Cain taken the time to explain what exactly 'heart's blood' entails?"

I set my fork down and took a sip of my enhanced water. Before setting the cup down, I held it up to look at it through the light. A clear cup of e-wat, held at the right angle, would show the small particles of nutrients and bioenhancing stimulants added to the water. While I would normally refuse, I decided if there was ever a time to be okay with stims, that was it.

As I held off answering Miles's questions, I toyed with a few different responses. I finally settled on "Cain and I are... were discussing it."

Miles winked, and I scowled.

I understood neither Miles's fascination with the two of us nor why he seemed to delight in tormenting Cain.

What I did understand, with a fierce protectiveness that startled even myself, was that whatever heart's blood truly was about, it was deeply personal between Cain and me. Our connection wasn't something I was going to chat about with someone like Miles.

I'd been hungry, but the food was already souring in my stomach. I pushed my plate away. "Off to the Celestial Plain, is it?"

"It is." Miles looked over at the door and beckoned.

I twisted around to see who had slipped into the room to find no one had, at least not yet. The door opened, and the two servers entered. Watchful eyes were everywhere, something useful to remember.

"We're finished," Miles said with a wave of his hand over the table. "My compliments to the chef, once again."

The men bowed and went to work clearing the dishes.

"Shall we?" Miles asked.

Miles reached out a hand but didn't fuss at my rejection. He took the lead, walking us through the command deck. Moving through a corridor was unnerving, with the feeling of déjà vu trailing after me. If Miles was aware of my discomfort, he didn't seem to care. He led me past Central Processing, and I couldn't help but shiver. I fought the all-too-fresh memories of my father's hologram and Mrs. Gol clamoring to be relived in the eerily familiar space.

I was so engrossed in not allowing the memories of the *Rapscallion* to overwhelm me that I didn't pay attention to how Miles was moving us through the ship. When we stopped, I realized I was lost and imagined Cain standing next to me, a scowl on his face with a sharp swish of his tail and a few cutting remarks on my lack of awareness at a critical time.

You have to keep your wits about you at a time like this. But the words echoed through my mind and only left me feeling hollow.

"Here we are." Miles flung his arms wide at the entrance to another room. "The repository of all things Star Eater or, as they prefer to call themselves, the Celestial Light."

18

Unexpected Revelations

At Miles's dramatic announcement, I half expected the door to open and reveal a room full of Star Eaters with darkened lighting and their mysterious forms swaying back and forth to the rhythm of some type of otherworldly music.

Alas. 'Twas not to be.

The doors slid open to reveal a cheerfully lit and rather spacious lab. Screens and workstations dotted the perimeter. In the center was a slowly rotating holo of a world with various symbols hovering above the various continents, and overlaid on top were latitude and longitude coordinates.

"Tracking or researching?" I asked as I stepped inside and looked around.

A few individuals were in the room, not in uniform, but each wore the same gray jumpsuit.

"A little of both," Miles responded. "Dr. Ashter, if you please."

I whipped around at hearing the name. "Dr. Si-Ial Ashter? *The* Dr. Si-Ial Ashter? Who unraveled the mysteries of the Three Heralds? And who opened up the deep-sea caves on Mandarin's Rhine?"

A man who appeared to be in his thirties, possibly even his late twenties, turned from his work and walked over. I had no doubt it was *the* Dr. Ashter, considering the amount of time I'd spent reading about him and seeing his pictures, but biologically, he was supposed to be in his nineties. Clearly, he'd been able to afford the very best in life extensions and bioupgrades.

Dr. Ashter had been born on Old Earth. All his biographers started by exploring his childhood fascination with the stars and his deep longing to explore unknown worlds. That was an important part of his life to take note of, for he'd been raised by a xenophobic mother who did everything she could to curtail his attempts to leave Old Earth.

His exploits, research, and pioneering work had made for popular tales when I was a kid—not just for the Orions but for most of the individuals who'd worked for my father. Every young xenologist dreamed of becoming the next Dr. Ashter, being a revolutionary voice in the field.

I was starstruck and may have drooled a little.

"I am he, and I have work to do," Dr. Ashter said.

"You always do," Miles replied with a smile. "Indulge us."

Dr. Ashter frowned. "It's your credits wasted."

"Ms. Orion needs to be brought up to speed concerning those of the Celestial Light," Miles said.

Dr. Ashter opened his mouth then snapped it shut. "Orion."

If I hadn't been in awe of the man, I would've caught the hint of scorn in how he pronounced my name.

"I knew an Orion once."

I caught the distaste that time. I wiped the foolish grin off my face and crossed my arms against my chest. "So?"

Dr. Ashter shook his head. "Pity. Come."

When we'd taken no more than a few steps toward the holo filled with stars and worlds, the room severely tilted to the right, something that shouldn't happen on a warship or, really, any ship in this day and age. Layers upon layers of coding, engineering ingenuity, circuits, backup systems, and science beyond my understanding had all been developed with the express purpose of allowing a ship's occupants to continue working or fighting, no matter what maneuvers the ship had to take.

Yet there we were. Supposedly on one of the finest warships ever created, we all tumbled or slid toward the wall as our orientation in space changed. The soft yellow lighting switched to the harsh glare of red seconds before we lost gravity.

Anything and anyone not secured to the floor floated.

Thankfully, I'd been through my fair share of drills. I reached out and grabbed hold of the nearest stationary object, the corner of a workstation. Holding on with one hand, I pulled my legs in close and switched on my boot's mag-locks. Without a lot of grace, I pulled and twisted until my feet were close enough for the mag-locks to engage. I experienced a brief moment of conflict within my body as the lack of gravity wanted to lift me from the floor, but my boots held me firmly in place.

I'd expected a smidgen of panic. That type of thing

wasn't supposed to happen, and I was in a room full of scientists and researchers. But I should have known better. Everyone else had engaged their mag-lock boots, and Dr. Ashter was calmly issuing orders as Miles moved toward the door.

Trying to run in mag-lock boots feels like wading through a time dilution filled with swamp sand while a hundred-mile wind pushes against you. Despite my enormous dislike of moving faster than a snail's pace in mag-locks, I caught up to Miles.

"What's going on?" I asked at the same time I realized he was talking to someone else.

He was sporting an integrated comms unit, the improved idea over the hardwired comm sleeves. With the amount of credits at his disposal, I highly doubted he had any issues with the tech like the unfortunate men and woman on the *Rapscallion* had.

"They fired on us?" Miles asked. That was the first time I'd seen his mask slip. "Are you sure you have the correct ID numbers?"

I trailed after Miles as he made his way back to command, deciding to keep my mouth shut.

First of all, I didn't want to interrupt him as even half a conversation is more information than nothing at all. Second, I wasn't sure he even realized I was following, and if I made a big stink, he probably would've had some hulk of a bodyguard forcibly remove me, just out of spite.

If I'd learned anything about the strange man, it was that he liked his riddles even more than Mrs. Gol. I didn't think a potential space battle was going to change his need to be the one holding all the cards.

Miles's questions continued as we entered command. I slipped off to one side and tried to make myself as innocuous as possible.

To the untrained eye, the room appeared to be in utter chaos. Officers darted back and forth between stations as questions and commands were shouted throughout the room. After having spent nearly a year in IGJ custody and being exposed to a handful of emergency situations, I knew the officers madly dashing back and forth were confirming intel and racing to keep their captain and employer updated.

"On screen," the captain barked.

The view screens covering the wall opposite the one I was trying so hard to blend into flared to life. The drab grays of the metallic panels were replaced by a resplendent view of space. If we hadn't been on the verge of some serious battle situation, the view would've been worth sitting down and admiring.

Lunar 5 was built on a moon roughly the same size as Old Earth's moon. From our vantage point, the light from the system's sun reflected off the moon's surface at just the right angle to illuminate the base. The tall spires of the administration district caught the sunlight and added to the myriad of stars twinkling in the vastness of space.

Orbiting the moon were three different IGJ checkpoints, and coming off those were several styles and classes of ships. Long-haul suppliers were strung out in lines, all waiting to pass through the IGJ checkpoints. A few personal craft were tucked here and there in the lines, and I spied at least one corporate ship from the

Goldsmith Consortium. I didn't have stellar eyesight, but the gold-plated exterior was a dead giveaway of the Consortium's bold flaunting of their wealth.

All that took a back seat to an IGJ security ship, though. The vessel wasn't one of the small security patrol ships, either, but if I was guessing correctly, it was the largest class of ship the IGJ deployed. Anything bigger, and we would have been staring down the barrel of another warship.

The security ship's gun turrets were pointed at us, and I had no doubt their weapons system was locked on to the *Samaritan*. I'd read the standard IGJ pamphlets and promotional material they'd put out after the last upgrade of their fleet. Technically, the media scooped the story of how the IGJ had bought up a plethora of blossom missiles and promptly outfitted their larger vessels with the deadly weapons.

Those missiles were a combination of human ingenuity and Jumjul genius. Blossoms boasted a ninety-percent success rate of incapacitating or destroying their target. Notably, Jumjul vessel stats weren't included in the pamphlets.

The missile encapsulated fifty-three smaller missiles, which when fired, broke apart and blossomed into randomized patterns capable of shifting and changing accordingly to their target's movements. That made defensive maneuvering almost an impossibility.

My personal theory was that the IGJ leaked the information to the media in order to create a buzz as a deterrent. Nobody would want to take on that type of weapon.

Space was vast, a multifaceted place full of billions upon billions of individuals of multiple species with widely differing opinions, cultures, and religious out-looks, an easy place for conflicts to be sparked, all of which might require the IGJ to intervene.

All that translated into the fact that the IGJ had made their fair share of enemies and, in turn, was a powerful enemy as well.

"Captain Dabrowski, if you please." Miles motioned for her to step onto the dais.

"We're beyond my authority, sir. Chatter says you've been recognized," Captain Dabrowski replied.

With a tight-lipped nod of understanding, Miles took her place.

"Comms," Miles politely ordered as if he had decided a dessert course was needed after all he had eaten.

"Comms are open sir," a young Telt replied, its yel-low-and-orange-hued fur frizzed out in an uncontrollable biological reflex to intense situations.

"This is Zhu Akio of the House Zhu, brother to the estimable, austere Diamond of the Sea, the emperor of—"

"We are well aware of who you are," someone cut in. "Stand down and be prepared to be boarded."

"Well, that's rather rude," Miles said with a shake of his head. "Flip over to visual."

I supposed if trying to impress with his wealth and status wasn't going to work, he would rather play the madman.

The screen changed to display the looming face of a middle-aged man. His skin bore several minute scars, and his right eye was clouded. His sandy-brown hair had been buzzed, and his position in relation to the cameras revealed the top of a tightly buttoned-up dress jacket.

He was a man who wasn't going to play games.

"Perhaps you're new to patrol?" Miles asked.

"You have two minutes to comply. Take any further action or disregard the order, and I will fire."

"I have a standing arrangement with the IGJ. A bit of work on the side, so to speak. Perhaps you need to check in with your commanding officer?" Miles asked as he held up a hand to inspect his fingernails. "I'll wait."

With his focus shifted to feigning indifference, he missed the victorious smirk on the man's face. "My orders come directly from the commandant herself."

Miles sighed. "Very well. Captain, shall we show this unfortunate soul exactly what we are—"

The man rudely interrupted Miles once more. "Perhaps this might change your mind."

His image shrank as he stepped back and allowed us to see all of him, a good portion of his ship's command deck, and an individual on his knees, upper body hunched over, a gun pointed at his head.

"Cain," I whispered.

19

InterGalactic Portion-Sized Complications

I stared in horror. *My annoying, infuriating* IGJ *agent.*

Two words leaped to mind: "heart's blood." While I couldn't spout an official definition as to what all they encompassed, I was beginning to have a vague notion of what they meant.

Our connection wasn't miraculously restored, but as those two words moved through my thoughts, Cain raised his head, and I would've sworn he stared straight at me.

I tried to stifle my cry of alarm as I looked at him, but I couldn't.

I've seen individuals bloodied after a fight. During one dark period in my life, I frequented jump fights. Perhaps watching had been cathartic on some level. I wasn't sure as I hadn't been getting along with my therapist at the time.

I pushed off the wall and moved down to the captain's dais to stand next to Miles.

One of Cain's eyes was completely swollen shut, and dried blood ringed his nose and the corners of his lips. His jacket was gone, and the vest and shirt underneath were ripped and soiled with blood and Jupiter only knew what else.

"Make a note of visual confirmation the suspect Mahia Orion is on board the *Samaritan* as well," the man ordered to someone off-screen.

"An unfortunate turn of events," Miles said as he stretched to his full height, "but if you keep up to date on local gossip, you'll find this particular IGJ isn't on my invite list to the Emperor's Ball this year. So I'm not quite sure how putting him on display is any type of deterrent."

"And yet, I do believe you have use for him, do you not?" the man replied.

"Perhaps. But I can find uses for even the nastiest pieces of garbage," Miles countered.

"What do you want?" I asked.

Miles threw me a stern look, and I ignored him. I didn't care about Miles's games or the banter that might lead to some type of arrangement. Cain was right there. I needed to know what had to happen to get him back.

The other man's eyes moved to study me, and after a deep breath and slow exhalation, he asked, "What do I want? To bring criminals to justice"—he leveled a stare at me—"by any means necessary."

"Cut it," Miles ordered. After comms were shut down, he turned toward me. "You foolish child. Have you not paid attention to anything I've been trying to tell you?"

"All you've told me are a bunch of circular logic

riddles and probably a few misdirects thrown in for fun," I all but shouted.

"I can see why Wats left you behind. You're not cut out for this at all," Miles snapped. "He should have looked to his son before you."

I blinked and stumbled off the dais. "What did you just say?"

"Get her off my command deck," Miles ordered.

The individuals under his command didn't hesitate. Two officers to my left moved toward me, their hands hovering above the weapons holstered at their hips. My eyes darted around the room, seeking any advantage or avenue of escape. I found nothing helpful.

But as I turned to back away from those officers, my peripheral vision caught two others moving away from their stations. *It's not like I can make a run for it. A bit of overkill, don't you think?* I wondered what they thought I was going to do.

The two who had backed away from their stations reached up and touched something on their upper sleeves, and a far deadlier version of a Vulture-class weapon sprang to life on each. Within seconds, the weapons did what they'd been designed to do.

The officers closest to them died first, and as everyone scrambled in the confusion of who was fighting whom, it was all too late.

Someone shoved me out of the way, and I crumpled down into an awkward kneeling posture. I don't know who it was or what they were trying to do, but they saved my life. The captain's chair exploded. Debris flew through the air, and the force was enough to break my boots' magnetic connection. Before I could aimlessly float through the fighting, I heard a pop, and gravity was restored. I hit the floor and landed next to Captain Dabrowski.

I tried to get into a better position and turned the woman over to assess the damage. My hands came away covered in blood oozing from a gaping wound in her chest. No amount of bioupgrades could've helped with something like that.

I squeezed my eyes shut at the horrific sight but opened them when I felt a hand grab my wrist. I'm not sure I'll ever understand how that captain was still alive, but her head turned toward me, and she held my gaze with a few seconds of clarity in her crystal-blue eyes. Her other hand moved toward me, her fingers curled into a tight fist.

"Take it," she murmured as blood poured from her mouth. Then she blinked and was gone.

Without giving a thought about the fighting still going on around me, I pulled her fingers open and stared at a small edible t-square—banned tech.

Edible tech had been invented off the back of Jumjul biology. One of the reasons behind their military might and general badassery was, in large part, due to genetic memory. Out of all the known species, they were the only ones with that particular quirk.

Humans, Glipglows, and Welpies alike had all gone to work on crafting some type of tech to mimic that idea—not passing down entire genetic lineages but preselected memories or genetic coding beneficial to the recipients. But when the tech was close to being finalized, governments and others in power put a stop to it—too much fear about classified information or long-buried secrets coming to light, not to mention the stern dislike the Jumjul had to anyone trying to mimic their advantage.

I popped that sucker in my mouth and swallowed. *I know.*

The t-square could have contained anything from innocuous childhood memories to genetic coding for an incurable disease. The captain could also have thought I was someone else, but those few seconds while she was staring straight at me, I didn't get that impression. It had been an offering from a captain of a ship that shouldn't have existed, run by a man who knew far more than he was letting on.

You bet your shiny rockets I swallowed the t-square.

Unfortunately, the whole experience was a letdown, no miraculous bursts of data or insight. I didn't have a sudden urge to jump up and help in the fight.

Instead, as I knelt there in disappointment, a pair of hands wrapped themselves around my arms, twisted, and hauled me to my feet. *Oh goodie. The bad guys have established comms again.*

"We're secure, sir," the man holding me reported.

"Good. Lower shields, and we'll send over transport."

"And the rest of the ship?"

"Flash the images of their dead captain and command crew, plus a good shot of their employer in restraints. There won't be much trouble."

"Yes, sir."

My arms were yanked behind me, and restraints were

slapped on my wrists. Once I was secure, a hand pushed on my shoulder and forced me back to my knees.

"Make up your mind, will you?" I muttered.

My little comment earned me a slap across the back of the head, which brought back some rather unpleasant memories from my previous entanglement with the IGJ.

I couldn't stop the question. "Were you assigned to the *Sunburst* a few years back?"

I didn't receive another physical reminder to color within the lines, but I did receive a growl and a verbal threat that if I moved or tried anything, I would be shot. *Surprise, surprise.*

The two IGJ plants—or ship's traitors, I wasn't yet sure of anything other than them being chunks of waste garbage—moved from workstation to workstation, following their orders, sealing off the decks and lowering shields.

As the two men worked, I glanced over at Miles and was relieved to find he was still alive. Untrustworthy though he was, he was the best ally I had at the moment. *Barely, though.*

A fairly good trickle of blood was running down the side of his face, which I surmised originated from a rather nasty blow to the head. I watched him and silently willed him to look up at me, to give me any hint of what to do or any assurance he had the situation under control. *A tall order.*

To my dismay, the man groaned, his head drooped forward, and he toppled over.

"Shit," one of the men muttered. He rushed over and completed a quick bioscan. "He needs medical."

"He'll get it when we make it back to the *Justus*."

A bit pretentious on the name. I wisely kept that little thought to myself.

I knelt in silence for quite some time as my brain spun through an endless array of possibilities, each a tad bit wilder and more unlikely as I went along. Also, I was carrying more tech inside my body than I ever had before. I hadn't forgotten about the pesky smart bots coursing through my blood nor the fact that the plans Miles and the Star Eaters had for me had been seriously derailed.

I should've considered the consequences of ingesting the edible t-square. For example, I didn't know if a mini war would be going on inside me, smart bots versus t-square. I really hoped I wouldn't find out. Or maybe I could at least sell tickets to the fight and make a tidy profit before I turned into a mutant or something.

"Sir," someone said from behind me.

I couldn't help but wonder how the rest of the ship's crew had fared, if they'd put up a fight or surrendered. I also wondered what had happened to Dr. Ashter. Anyone who followed his work or had a chance to read through the stories surrounding him would know he'd been in worse scrapes than that and always found a way to survive. But death had a way of catching up to those who cheat it too many times. I just hoped That wasn't the end of his career. The man was a genius xenologist.

"Orders up. This ship has been secured, and the *Justus* has established a functional transfer hub. Once the prisoners have been transferred to the *Justus*, we'll slave the *Samaritan* to its systems and tow it along with us. A skeleton crew is to remain behind… and get this one some medical treatment. I'd personally like to see him bleed out for all the trouble he's caused me, but it won't do to have the brother of the emperor die in our custody."

That tidbit was useful. Even if the man didn't appear to care about me directly, knowing he was concerned about something was helpful.

Merciful Saturn's rings. I'd forgotten about Cain's nano-bots. I didn't care if I was about to earn another slap or ten more. "Hey. You. Tell your superior that they need to make sure—"

I never got the chance to finish my question. Flashes of light obscured my vision as the IGJ agent hauled me to my feet. I blamed Miles and his underhanded trick with the Star Eaters.

Why, universe? Why me?

20

The Art Thief

As I was losing touch with my physical body, I still had the faint notion of walking. My weight subtly shifted from side to side as I continued to press one foot onto the floor while the other lifted and moved forward. I felt the agent's fingers digging into my arm, and I could still smell the sweaty, musky scent of bodies that had been in uniforms for too long.

But the flashes of light grew stronger and longer until nothing was left but an awareness of being devoured by the brilliant white light surrounding me. Everything else melted away. I turned my head to the right then to the left, but everywhere I looked, I was met with only light.

The sensation was like piloting a ship edging ever closer to a sun, minus being vaporized and all that jazz. As I crept forward, light and warmth engulfed me. But at that moment, all I could see and feel was the sun, right before I would wink out of existence. But oddly enough, the light didn't blind me or burn me to a crispy critter, no matter what the rational part of my brain was trying to tell me.

I lifted what I perceived was an arm, and the light rearranged itself to flow around my skin. A small giggle escaped at the sheer exhilaration of it all. My mind believed I was swimming through liquid sunlight, and I relished how it slid over my skin until I was cocooned within its embrace.

I didn't try to question what was happening or think of a logical explanation. All my worries, fears, and anxieties were gone. Utter peace moved through me.

Then, in the distance, the light dimmed, and a shadow moved. The darkness slunk its way forward, but it wasn't a shadow, merely an absence of light.

I experienced no fear, only curiosity. The darkness twisted and turned and grew with every inch of distance it covered. The light shifted and made way for the darkness, and I sensed a third presence nestled within the dark shroud.

A tendril of darkness spun forward, thinning as it stretched toward me. When its inquiring touch was only millimeters from what I perceived to be my fingertip, the light and the darkness vanished.

I felt as if I was falling from a great height, my fingers and toes tingling as awareness returned to my body. My eyes flew open as panic ripped through me, and I flailed and thrashed, only to discover I hadn't been falling at all but was lying on the cold hard floor of a detention cell.

My chest heaved as I gasped for air and tried to gain my bearings. That didn't take long, as the scene was all too familiar. A not so comfortable or clean cot was bolted to both the floor and the wall, tucked up in a corner. An outdated Dash 'n' Wash station sat to my right, and the distinct hum of a force field generator filled the air.

When the IGJ had detained me after everything went down with my father, I started off in a similar detention cell. After a few months, they upgraded me to a small hab-unit, still under guard, but they had at least ascertained I wasn't a threat or a flight risk. I'd been scared out of my mind and had cooperated the best I knew how for those early months.

You can bet your credit rating I wasn't going to be so compliant this time around.

I tried to stand, but my legs were like heavy weights, and the movement caused my heart to race. Maybe I'd been drugged.

And what in Jupiter's moons did I see? It was too bizarre to have been a hallucination and too coincidental not to be wrapped up with whatever the Star Eaters had done or with Miles—or both.

One thing was certain: I felt the absence of the light as keenly as I felt the absence of Cain. I shivered despite my well-padded jumpsuit, and all my jumbled emotions were back. The blissful feeling of peace was gone.

But what does it mean?

I didn't know, and I wasn't given any time to ponder life's questions as the force field abruptly dropped, and two armed IGJ agents stepped into view.

"Get up," the man snapped.

Using the little strength I had left, I got to my feet and swayed. My hand shot out to press against the wall in an effort to steady myself.

"Don't try anything stupid. We have orders to shoot first and ask questions later," the woman said, sneering.

"Seems a bit backward," I muttered.

"Get moving," the man said.

I took a deep breath and concentrated on moving one foot then the other. I really thought a cold, dank, dark interrogation room was in my future. Instead, I was soon sitting in a rather comfortable chair and was treated to a view of some pieces of art bolted to the walls. I hadn't pegged the man as an art lover.

He wasn't.

A woman, who stepped into the room and snapped her finger to dismiss the two guards and sat down behind the sleek metallic desk, was the art lover. The man who'd done all the talking hadn't been kidding. His orders had come directly from the commandant.

I recognized her from all the times her image was splashed across the media, either praising her for her ingenious execution of IGJ resources or lambasting her as the worst commandant in IGJ history. *No breaks for the people in power.*

"It appears medical cleared you except for the small issue of what appears to be smart bots coursing through your blood. Can you explain that?"

Commandant Hazine Yilmaz studied me with her dark-brown eyes. Her face was framed by an abundance of black curls, and judging from the way she sat, shoulders pulled back and fingers interlaced and resting atop her desk, she was quite comfortable with her position of power.

"Nope," I said. "But I would be curious to know what happened to one of your agents. A Jorge Silone-Ruger? Seems there's been a bit of a misunderstanding with my former employees over my relationship with the man."

"Clarify your use of the word *misunderstanding.*"

I arched an eyebrow at her cavalier response. "The contract Confore put out on me? Obviously, there was some kind of mix-up, that they believed I was connected to Jorge. Who, by the way, was researching the SeeClear hardware upgrades. Care to shed any light on that?"

"Care to share any light on your smart bots?"

I frowned. *All right, lady.* "You first. Tell me about Project Clear Sight, and I'll tell you about the smart bots."

Yilmaz tilted her head and regarded me with shrewd eyes. "Perhaps my other guest would be willing to share information. I do believe he is in a more precarious situation than you are, isn't that correct?"

"Cain," I whispered.

"Yes?" the commandant replied.

"Cain." I looked at her, and my chest tightened. "If you know about the nanobots, then help him. If they're not deactivated in time, they'll kill him."

She didn't move. She didn't smile or even bat an eyelash.

"I will ask again. Can you explain the abundance of smart bots in your blood?"

"Didn't you just hear what I said?" I said and felt the prick of something sharp at the bottom of my neck.

The deceptively beautiful chair morphed into a prisoner's nightmare. The armrests rearranged themselves into restraints while the two front legs did the same.

And that prick of pain in my neck was no doubt some form of the latest designer drugs the IGJ, clandestine government intelligence corps, and high-end crime rings used to make their prisoners a little more cooperative.

I clamped my mouth shut. I wasn't up for a heart-to-heart with the lady.

Unfortunately, the drugs didn't help.

"I did. But Mr. Turen ed-Suren isn't high on my priority list at the moment." The commandant stared at me. "I find it curious. The daughter of a known terrorist, who I'm presuming you understand did far worse than aiding the Eeri in destroying some of our bases, is found with the same smart bots her father worked to eradicate."

Remember when I mentioned the worst was yet to come? That was the worst yet to come. Right there. Right then. And it knocked out all my other concerns.

I laughed at first. "Right. Nice try. But I'll give you a nine out of ten for a zinger of an opening statement."

Commandant Yilmaz leaned back with a knowing smile. "Let me be frank with you, Mahia. I don't have time to waste on cryptic intelligence gathering or clandestine interrogation techniques. I need to know whatever you know. And I need to know it now."

Adding my guilty pleasure of watching true-crime dramas to the time I'd spent with the IGJ, I felt as if I'd experienced the entire wide variety of interrogation techniques the IGJ had to offer. To my surprise, that was a new one.

My shoulders dropped, and my body relaxed into the comfort of the chair. *Thanks, designer drugs.*

"I don't know what you're talking about," I said. Admittedly, my words were a little slurred, but they were still the truth despite the fact that Miles had lied to me about the whole message deal. I would never have considered that little revelation.

But thanks to the drugs, I did feel an urgent need to clarify a few things. "I'm aware of what my father did, what actually got him arrested. Thanks to the evil little lady."

Yilmaz raised an eyebrow. "Are you referring to Mrs. Fairhaven Gol?"

"That's the one," I said. "Evil little dermatex."

"And what did Mrs. Gol tell you?"

"Not much," I started then was distracted by the art hanging on the wall. "Those look strangely familiar to me."

"Mahia, I need you to focus."

"Classic styles never go out of fashion, do they." I wasn't entirely sure what I was saying, only that I needed to keep talking about the artwork for some reason. "Everyone always wants a piece of the classics. Doesn't matter where they come from, really. Art is art."

I leaned forward as far as the chair's restraints would allow. "I recognize that one. Hold on." *If only I had some smart glass like Miles did. Then I could reach out and pull up some... That's it. Holy smokes.* "That's a piece from the Three Heralds. Pretty impressive to casually display such an important piece of history as wall décor."

Yilmaz opened her mouth to continue with our little conversation, but my focus had already shifted to the next piece of art.

"Hmm. Not as familiar with the next piece," I said. "Broad brushstrokes combined with intricate geometrical shapes set against a backdrop of swirling clouds, dusted with…" I squinted. "With what, mica? Quite a beautiful image." It reminded me of something, but I couldn't place it at the moment.

The next piece was fragmented and preserved behind glass. Even though sections were missing, I recognized the work, *The Transcendence*, an early religious piece from Dar. Shove me out an air lock, I would never have thought the Darquets would've tolerated any of their works being taken off world. Either the commandant had done something outrageously heroic to be gifted such a piece, or she was a thief.

The last piece of art, off to the left, didn't ring any bells. It featured three strips of canvas. The first was solid black. The second was black again but had some type of iridescent overlay that shimmered when I moved my head. And the last piece of canvas had a center of yellow, which faded out to white.

"It does take a trained eye to spot pieces such as those," Yilmaz said with a bemused look.

I laughed and rolled my eyes back to the commandant. "I should hope so. I was trained by one of the best, you know."

The woman frowned and leaned back in her chair. "Wats Hawking Orion was one of the best. Top in his class, a darling of the higher echelons of society. He was expected to become the next worlds' renowned xenologist, plus a few other titles. What areas did he train you in?"

I squeezed my eyes shut then popped them open. My concentration was getting harder to maintain. I'm not sure what I told her, ramblings of the different places my father had carted us off to. Obscure lessons sprang to mind.

The commandant kept me talking about the places I'd been and the work I'd watched my father do until I felt a little of my control returning.

Looking back, I realized she was waiting for the worst of the drug's effects to clear. Someone must have been a little too eager to see me talk and upped the dose a tad bit too much.

"He sounds like he was a good father," she murmured.

"He was until he decided to just leave us. Get arrested and see his children's lives sucked into a black hole," I replied.

"Tell me about that. How did you feel when Mrs. Gol told you the truth? Do you hate your father now? Or do you see him as some type of hero? Standing up against the evil in the world when no one else would?"

The commandant was good but not quite good enough. She'd played her hand and lost the bet. Those were questions she never should've asked. Drugged or not, I wasn't going to give the answers she wanted, and the misfire helped clear some of the fog from my mind.

"The Three Heralds are priceless pieces of cultural history. You must have paid a pretty penny to get your hand on them."

Yilmaz nodded.

My eyes kept swinging back to the second piece of art. *Have I seen it somewhere before? But where?* I knew it was recent. *Epsilon's Station?* No, I didn't think so. *Lunar 5? Maybe in a store window? Certainly not on the docking platform.* Nothing had been there, not even the data records.

That hazy line of thinking led me to something else I knew I should ask since I'd been so graciously asked to sit and chat with the commandant. It had to do with Cain and the docking platform.

Oh, right. "Since I've been granted this rare opportunity to talk with the highest authority within the InterGalactic Justice system, I do have a question for you. Care to explain why the IGJ would decide to purge data when that's heavily frowned upon by the Jumjul High Court?"

The commandant didn't flinch. "If you have a suspected case of illegal data purging, then I urge you to file a report. But I warn you, caseloads have become rather heavy at the moment, and an agent may get back to you only within a few months' time. By then, I suspect, everyone will have moved on from whatever issue you may believe there to be."

"So a good old-fashioned cover-up, then?"

Yilmaz smiled. "No. Just doing my sworn duty."

The game was a draw. *Fudge nuggets.* An out-and-out confession would have been fantastic, but all the nefarious characters had aced their cryptic-speech classes.

She laughed. "I see your father in you. And"—she leaned forward—"that's a compliment... this time."

21

It's All about the Leverage

I secretly hoped that, after our friendly little chat, the commandant would be finished with me for a good long while. I needed time for my head to clear, to mull over what she hadn't said more than what she had. And I was praying she'd taken me seriously about Cain's nanobots. Surely, she wouldn't just let him die. She'd hinted at how he might be helpful to her line of questioning. But maybe she would just shove him out an air lock when the final countdown started.

Instead of me being given at least a few hours to consider how my life was rapidly careening off course, a different set of guards arrived a few minutes later. *Great. I bet she's passing me off to someone who specialized in interrogation techniques.*

Instead, my guards escorted me to a narrow room, and the first thing I saw was two rows of theater-type seating.

Without thinking, I said, "Oh goodie, date night. Do I get popcorn with the show?"

That earned a grunt from the guards, who turned and

secured the door. Annoyed, I turned around to realize what I'd thought had been a dormant screen was actually a window overlooking a surgical center.

My heart leaped into my throat, and I pressed myself up against the glass as I stared down at the main attraction. Illuminated by a halo of light, laid out on a medical platform, was Cain. His arms were extended and secured to wings off the platform, and I noted the same type of restraints around his ankles. *Is he dead? Have we passed the expiration limit on the nanobots?* No, I didn't think so. I doubted that much of his body would be left if we had.

"Cain!" I yelled and pounded against the glass in the vain hope I was strong enough to break through it. When that didn't work, I turned and tried to pry one of the chairs off the riser, but it was securely bolted down.

I turned back to the window and screamed, hoping Cain could at least hear me and know I was there, trying to get to him. A jolt of electricity raced through me, and I fell to the floor, my muscles convulsing from the high dosage.

"I'm afraid we don't have any popcorn," Commandant Yilmaz calmly quipped.

I looked up at the woman and spoke through gritted teeth. "I thought you weren't one for clandestine interrogation techniques?"

"Oh, I'm not. But as I mentioned, I'm on a tight schedule. Since the drugs didn't do what I needed, I'm reasoning this method will be the most expedient," she said as she stepped over me. "Get her up."

One of the guards lunged forward and hauled me to my feet.

"If you provide answers I don't like or are off tar-get"—she turned to stare at me—"you'll receive another electrical shock. The voltage will increase each time I'm forced to use it. Subsequently, Mr. Turen ed-Suren, will be subjected to… those pesky clandestine interrogation techniques you mentioned."

Forgive me, but I found myself wishing I was dealing with Mrs. Gol instead of that calm, rational woman. I could keep crazy off-balance, but the commandant was in charge of the largest multifaceted organization of different species in the known worlds. I had no doubt in my mind that she'd earned the position instead of getting it as a political favor or some such nonsense.

I felt nothing but hatred for the commandant, whereas Mrs. Gol had earned at least a smidgen of sympathy because of her son, Triton.

And at least Mrs. Gol had given me several chances to try to cooperate. If you want to, label her as a mad hatter for scheming that way, but the commandant had gone straight for the throat. She'd automatically assumed I wouldn't be cooperative.

I wouldn't say she was wrong, but she didn't give me much of a chance. And no, I wouldn't count trying to drug me into compliance as a chance. But maybe I would've reconsidered a few things if she'd at least faked a bit of compassion and helped out with some answers.

I turned back to the window and stared at Cain. His eyes were closed, and I couldn't tell if he was breathing. I assumed he was. Any other option wasn't going to work for me.

"What about the nanobots?" I asked.

"Why have you been injected with the smart bots?" the commandant asked instead of answering my question.

"I don't care about those. I need to know if—" I was cut off as my unsatisfactory response earned me another jolt of electricity.

"Focus," the commandant said.

"Not until you assure me Cain is safe from the—"

She was determined not to let me finish.

"I can tell you that those nanobots are the least of Mr. Turen ed-Suren's concerns at the moment. Now, the smart bots?" the woman asked.

"I lost a bet," I replied.

She hadn't given me a solid answer, but at least it was an acknowledgment of the danger Cain was in.

Right on cue, she reached over and zapped me again. At least that time I was prepared for it and leaned against the glass to retain a little dignity and not fall to the floor again.

The commandant turned toward the window and pressed her hand against the glass, and a variety of options sprang to life. She pressed one of the choices and said, "Doctor."

From the shadows beyond Cain's medical platform stepped a human woman dressed in the stereotypical whites of the medical profession. Even though I couldn't see what she was holding, I knew what she was doing when the doctor pressed down on Cain's arm. Cain's eyes flew open, and while I couldn't hear the scream through the glass, I felt its terrible horror.

My fingers curled into fists, and I pounded on the glass in vain, screaming at the doctor to stop, but one of the guards stepped up, grabbed my wrists, and twisted my arms behind my back.

"Why have you been injected with smart bots?"

If I'd been alone, I would have endured the shocks. Or if the one on the platform had been Miles and not Cain, I might've stayed quiet a bit longer, just to see if I could expose some kind of weakness in the commandant, of course.

But this was Cain, my heart's blood. His pain was my pain. I could not, in good conscience, be the cause of his torture.

"I was told I was to deliver a message," I muttered.

"From whom and to whom?"

"A jumped-up crazy madman to a group of even loonier goons," I said without thinking.

The answering electric shock was a tad longer and a bit more intense. That time, it didn't just cause my muscles to spasm uncontrollably, but I also felt the hint of pain each subsequent shock promised.

"Doctor, if you please…"

I couldn't bear to look and turned my head to the side.

"Who sent the message, and who was to receive it?"

I sagged against the guard, who reached out to grab me once the shock wore off. I didn't owe any loyalty to Miles. "Miles High wanted to send it. He injected me with the smart bots. And I don't know the names of who was to retrieve the message."

Okay, that was a gamble. Unless Miles had spilled his guts, the commandant wouldn't know there wasn't a message. Maybe that would be enough to slow her down, enough to satisfy her and stop the insanity. But I also didn't lie. I didn't know the names of the two Star Eaters we'd met. Honestly, I didn't know if Star Eaters had names.

After a thoughtful pause, she asked the next question. "How do you know Miles High?"

That, I could answer with ease. "I don't. Just needed a ride off Epsilon's Station is all. Said if I delivered the message, he would provide the ship. Easy peasy."

"And you allowed him to inject you? Without asking any other questions?" A hint of condemnation tinged her voice.

I agreed with her. "I didn't have a choice," I grumbled, which was halfway true. If I'd put up a fight, Cain would have done his worst to try to get us out of there alive. And at the time, I hadn't realized the full extent of what Miles was capable of. If we'd fought back, I was quite sure one or both of us would've been dead.

"I suppose not," the commandant said. "Did you ever hear your father speak of the monarchy? Of Zhu Akio, the heir to the throne of Old Earth?"

"My father?" I asked. "I don't know. How am I supposed to remember—"

"Doctor."

Whatever the good doctor was doing to Cain happened at the same time I had my next round of electrical shock. Only that time, it wasn't just a step up from the previous setting. The commandant must have cranked the damned tech wide open. Pain ripped through my body, and I sank to the floor.

The commandant squatted beside me. "It's quite

simple. Either you remember your father discussing Zhu Akio, or you don't. Which is it?"

I shook my head.

Yilmaz frowned and studied me. "All right." She stood up. "One last question for now. What is your affiliation with the Star Eaters?"

I rolled my head to the side for a better look at the woman. "They helped me on the *Rapscallion*." That was as close to the truth as I wanted to get, and I hoped my answer would spare me from another shock.

It didn't. The pain exploded through my body, and as the aftershocks rolled through me, the guards hauled me to my feet and pressed me against the window. I tried to look away, but they held my head in place. I squeezed my eyes shut, but one of the guards pried them open.

The doctor had moved to the other side of the medical platform to reveal her handiwork. Blood splatter dotted the floor, the doctor's gown, and Cain's tattered clothes. At first, I couldn't tell what they'd done to him, but then I saw it.

The damned doctor had cut off his tail.

I screamed a long string of profanity and promises at the commandant as she merely stared at me. When I stopped to take a gulp of air, she took a step forward.

"I'm trusting you'll be a bit more cooperative in the future. Or else Mr. Suren ed-Turen will begin to lose more than a tail."

I lunged forward, but the guards prevented me from reaching the commandant.

"Take her back to her cell."

With the IGJ's rough-and-tumble policy, something solid struck the back of my head, and everything went quiet and dark except for a woman's soothing alto voice, clear as a bell, which echoed in my head before I lost consciousness.

[HOLD, PLEASE.]
Talk about irony.

22

Sam

I woke with a splitting headache to discover I was back in my cell and had at least been deposited on the bed instead of the floor. The throbbing in my head increased as I tried to sit up, and I decided lying still was the better option by far.

Have you ever been to a Telt percussion procession? I don't recommend it, at least not without high-quality earplugs. Most introductory courses providing an exploratory look at the various species with which humanity shares space only brush the surface of the cultural and societal differences.

Here's a fact little known except by those who work within the arts department at one of the better-funded schooling branches: Telt music only developed with one family of instruments, percussion. Anything which could be hit, shaken, or scraped had been turned into a percussive instrument at some point in Telt history.

My head felt as if I was reliving the experience of witnessing over a hundred performers march to a mismatched rhythm only a Telt could enjoy.

[CONNECTION WAS MOMENTARILY LOST. REESTABLISHING…]

If my head hadn't discouraged any sudden movement, I would've jumped out of bed at the unwelcome voice inside my head. Instead, all I managed was a groan and the question of what fresh interrogation techniques the IGJ were testing on me.

[CONNECTION HAS BEEN ENABLED. PLEASE PROCEED WITH UPLINK COMMANDS.]

Gingerly, I rolled over and wrapped the measly slip of a pillow around my head the best I could. The added pressure didn't help, but I just wanted the pounding in my head to stop. Whatever the IGJ was up to, I wanted no part in it. I'd never been the organization's number one fan, and I certainly wasn't going to start after what the commandant had done to Cain.

<Cain? Are you there?> I knew the effort was futile. Cain's telepathic presence hadn't returned despite the close proximity we'd briefly shared during the interrogation.

Yet I hoped that by some kind of miracle I would get an answer.

I didn't.

As I lay there, forced to listen only to myself on top of the Telt parade, I realized what an absolute fool I'd been.

Miles had been right, despite being an infuriating piece of trash.

All the time I'd spent on my own, keeping my head down and minding my own business, had only served to isolate me. Originally, that had been the point. I certainly didn't want to invite the attention of the media, gawkers, and hate mail enthusiasts after what went down with my father.

But I'd taken the isolation to the max. I hadn't been interested in cultivating any small circle of friends. I hardly kept up with the majority of news reports. I did hear the flashes that covered the juiciest pieces of gossip. Billboards, pop-up screens, and info dumps were hard to ignore in the sprawling metropolis of Original Luna. But I'd chosen to work, go home, and drown my sorrows and anxieties in true-crime dramas and jute-store stories.

Burying the proverbial head in the sand wasn't how I'd been raised. My father never shielded my brother or me from the politics surrounding his work. Lectures and teaching moments included questions concerning past or present political and cultural conflicts. Wherever my father's work took us, I'd been able to identify the major players and influencers in the area.

The art of understanding political intrigue was mastered by more than a few xenologists. The majority of the history they study wouldn't exist without such machinations. Uncovering ancient history or aiding in exploring a different species' culture meant a xenologist had to untangle the convoluted movements of the society. And if the researcher wanted to maintain adequate funding or score the top dig sites, understanding how to work the surrounding currents at the time was imperative.

But I'd been so focused on my grief, my feelings of betrayal, and my desire to be left alone that I'd refused to think about the real-life political intrigue my father had dealt with, let alone how his actions had rippled through the known worlds.

I'd lied to myself when I thought I'd listened to Miles when, in reality, I hadn't heard a thing—even if the man had spoken in unnecessary riddles.

So there I was, and Cain was out somewhere, bloodied, bruised, and mutilated by a group he'd put his faith in.

At that moment, all I wanted to do was to reach out to him, to comfort—

[PLEASE PROCEED WITH UPLINK COMMANDS.]

I'm not playing your games, I growled inwardly. I wasn't going to let the IGJ or Yilmaz in, no matter how hard they tried or innovative they became.

[NOW THAT THE CONNECTION HAS BEEN ENABLED AND ESTABLISHED, IF UPLINK COMMANDS AREN'T INITIATED WITHIN THIRTY SECONDS, THIS UPLINK WILL BE TERMINATED PER STANDARD OPERATING PROCEDURES, SECTION THIRTY-FOUR C, SUBSECTION THREE, PARAGRAPHS FOUR THROUGH SIX.]

I ignored the voice and tried to focus on what pieces of information I'd missed. I thought back to my conversations with Miles and berated myself for not paying closer attention.

Good grief, talk about not paying attention. I shot out of bed and deeply regretted that decision, but I stayed upright. What a double-stuffed fool I was.

Proceed with uplink commands, I thought.

[PLEASE STATE YOUR FULL NAME.]

Mahia Eimariana Orion.

[PLEASE STATE YOUR BIRTH ORIGIN DATE.]

2589 Old Earth Standard. Old Earth.

[Your network has been scanned. A connection can be established with your subcutaneous HalfLife biochip. If you choose to proceed, this uplink will render the false HalfLife data useless. Do you wish to proceed?]

Why the hell not? I thought with a shrug. I wasn't hiding who I was anymore.

[Please respond with either yes or no.]

Yes.

Despite the continued pounding in my head, I paced back and forth, waiting for the response. When it did come, I slapped a hand over my mouth to quell my shout of glee.

[Connection verified. Command input from Captain Irina Ivanova Dabrowski verified. Command of the Samaritan transferred to Mahia Eimariana Orion. Welcome to the Sam Network. Would you like to access the root menu?]

Holy Saturn's rings and Jupiter's moons. My impulsive, dumb decision had paid off. Remember the edible t-square I downed without a thought?

Biological encoded control of a ship, all within one glorious edible t-square—for the level of programming and coding that needed to be crammed into one small t-square, I was more than impressed at the success of such genius. I guessed that was the next generation of tech after the mishaps with the hardwired comm sleeves.

But it did beg the question: Why in the world had the captain given me access to her ship? Far better options were available, surely. Perhaps my assessment of her lucidity had been wrong. The captain could've thought I was someone else in the moment before she died, or maybe she'd been desperate to not allow her ship to fall under the command of the IGJ.

Either way, I didn't want to look the gift horse in the mouth, to borrow an Old Earth saying.

Yes. Bring up the root menu.

After a brief pause, the AI voice of the *Samaritan* worked her way through all the options. There were so many that I had to stop her before I got lost. Besides, I didn't have time to puzzle out all the intricate commands and tasks I could assign to the ship. That connection was my best chance at busting out of the IGJ and rescuing Cain.

If the commandant continued along her sadistic path of interrogation, I was sure Cain wouldn't be the only one who lost a few body parts. I don't know how the IGJ missed the edible tech in their scans, but I couldn't afford to have them going back and double-checking my bio readings.

Sam, can you break free from the IGJ *slave codes?*

[YES. BUT IT WILL REQUIRE A HARD-LINE CONNECTION.]

Fudge nuggets. No way would that be possible with me sitting in my cell. I needed access to a workstation.

Will any workstation on the IGJ *ship work?* I thought.

[YES.]

All righty.

"I'll talk." I knew my simple statement would get the response I needed.

The wait wasn't long before two agents appeared.

Oddly enough, I was thankful for my pounding

headache as I was marched through the ship. All I had to do was concentrate on the pain focused along my eyes and my jaw to keep my excitement and apprehension hidden. Bluffing had never been my strong suit. My father always said I broadcast my emotions like a Neetho hive mind.

The little stunt I'd pulled with Mrs. Gol in the abandoned medical facility had been a warm-up act. As I was taken back to the commandant's office, I conjured up the image of Cain lying on that medical platform, his tail discarded to one side. With that horrific image added to my headache, the tears slipping down my cheeks were quite real as I was shoved down into a chair. No bluffing was necessary.

23

Unexpected (and Unwelcome) Correspondence

"Lieutenant, see to it that Captain Clearmont is brought up to speed on the hardware disbursements. Our time-table has sped up," Commandant Yilmaz said as she walked into her office. "Corporal, return to your posting. You're both dismissed."

Each of my escorts snapped a pithy "sir" and left.

Despite the popular plot choice of the hero taking action when the guards are dismissed in jute-store novels, I quietly stayed seated. I didn't have military combat training and wasn't about to jeopardize the one shot I did have.

"A sensible decision," Commandant Yilmaz commented as she took her seat.

I wasn't sure if she was talking about my choice to talk or the fact I didn't try to rush her. Either way, I didn't like her chummy tone.

Feigning defeat, I looked up at the woman then hastily lowered my eyes. "I have…" I added in a good sniffle or two. "One request." Then in a beautifully perfect desperate whisper, I said, "Please."

"I'm not surprised. Go on."

"I want to… I need to see Cain. Please. Not through a piece of glass. I want to stand next to him and make sure he gets the medical attention he needs. Cain doesn't have anything to do with what you're looking for. He was just following orders in trying to keep me alive because of the contract Confore put out."

The request was a bold move but legitimate on all levels. I truly wanted to see Cain, and he needed medical attention, something I had no doubt he was receiving the bare minimum of.

That was my legitimate attempt to gain access to a workstation. And if it worked, then Sam could go to work. I had no idea what that meant, though. I wasn't that far along in the planning stages yet.

"Technically, those are two requests. But before I decide, I'm curious. What will you do if I refuse to grant them?"

Game point to you.

My brain scrambled, and I settled on the truth. I looked up and stared straight at her. "Make you take me apart piece by piece, looking for whatever it is you want." No bluffing there—I meant every word of it.

"Interesting." Yilmaz studied me as she leaned back in her chair and pursed her lips, her gaze never wavering from mine. "Mr. Turen ed-Suren has become more than a bodyguard, I gather."

Well… fudge. I hadn't considered how easily that supposition could be retrieved from what I'd just said.

"I'll accept your terms." She leaned forward and pressed a comm button on her desk. "See to it that Mr. Turen ed-Suren is taken to the medical bay." Then she turned her attention back to me. "But first, you'll answer a few questions before I grant the rest of your request."

I let out a breath I hadn't realized I'd been holding and gave a tense nod.

"We acquired an interesting piece of information from your lawyers, Bloodhearst and Strobe, if I'm not mistaken," the commandant stated.

Oh, Pluto's dilemma… This isn't good. I'd pushed that little tidbit to the back burner while we were dealing with the Project Clear Sight debacle.

"They are your lawyers, are they not?"

"Yes," I replied.

"Pressure, applied at just the right places, is effective at getting people to compromise their morals, but… I commend your choice of lawyers. Despite our use of the full brunt of IGJ resources, the personnel at Cleary Station didn't give up the information willingly."

I swallowed bile. I didn't need her to tell me any more to understand.

"What's your question?" I asked, trying to keep my voice as even as I could.

"First, I would like you to read through what we were able to acquire. Then I'll ask the questions."

The commandant touched the controls on her desk, and a screen appeared between us. The file opened, and my first instinct was to look away—partly because I didn't want to give the commandant the satisfaction of watching my real-time reaction to reading the missive and also partly because I wasn't ready to see what messages my father had left me.

One would think I would learn that I couldn't afford to ignore what was going on. I had to tread out into those nasty shock waves.

With one deep breath and a pounding heart, I sat up in the chair and read what was on the screen.

My little Eima,

If you're reading this letter, then I'm more than likely dead. I know it's a rather cliché way to begin a letter, but it's the truth. I understand how that word may strike a chord in you, as evidence from this letter suggests the truth is in the eye of the beholder. I assure you it is not.

Truth is a constant. As timeless as the underground murals on Isoth.

This letter must be brief, and I apologize. But the Celestial Plain must be included first, or everything that follows will only be mired in the waste bogs of Mandarin's Rhine.

Popular opinion has shifted, and by the time you read this, my extrapolations will be moot. I can only hope you'll have an easier time at rendering the silent wall of watchers than I have.

I would tell you to be careful and take care of yourself, but you were always running off into danger. So, all I can say is to please be aware. Sinkholes and false floors abound everywhere.

Pops.

I sat in stunned silence. I hadn't known what to expect, maybe an outright explanation as to why my father had done what he did or perhaps a confession of what he'd been a part of his whole life and kept secret. I didn't know, but I hadn't expected that.

"It makes for interesting reading. I would appreciate your interpretation," Yilmaz calmly stated.

I pushed myself back into the chair, as far away from the screen as I could get. "My father never told me what he was involved in, if that's what you're hoping for," I stated.

"I surmised as much from our previous conversations. Yet, you did promise to talk in exchange for some time with Mr. Turen ed-Suren," Yilmaz countered.

I had, and I knew whatever I was going to say had to be good enough to convince her I was telling the truth. I snorted and shook my head with a half smile. I needed to be like my father, who'd obviously been a deft hand at lying.

I sat up and looked her square in the eye. "I lost all respect for my father the moment I learned the truth on the *Rapscallion*. He was a man who lied to me and left me, as the IGJ should be all too aware. Then, even after he's dead, he reaches out and gets me caught up in a situation I don't understand and, frankly, don't want to."

I scooted forward. "This letter only confirms that he was mad. The only thing I can explain is his reference to the Celestial Plain. I don't know why or how, but he got messed up with the Star Eaters along the way. They helped me out with Mrs. Gol, as I mentioned earlier, and for some reason, seem to be working with Miles High.

"I was to deliver the message to the Star Eaters in exchange for transport to Lunar 5. I met with two Star Eaters, who threw a wrench in the works, and then you and your little crew interfered with your poorly staged attempt at flushing out Miles with Cain's abduction. Which, all things considered, doesn't add up. What's your end goal in all this? Shouldn't you be on my side?"

"I believe you've already answered that question." Yilmaz smiled unkindly.

Another point to you.

"Fine." I stood up and held out my arms. "Why don't you just extract the little suckers and be done with it? If there's a connection between Miles, my father, and the Star Eaters, then perhaps it's in there."

"We tried," the commandant replied, deflating my little show of dramatics. "But it seems your particular brand of smart bots is a cut above the ones on the black market. We need to approach the issue from a different direction if I deem it necessary to keep you alive."

"Then talk it over with Miles. He was the one who put them there in the first place."

"Don't worry. We will continue to make use of the would-be emperor."

I didn't like the sound of that even if Miles wasn't on my top-ten list—or even twenty.

That old saying, "The enemy of my enemy is my friend," could've worked both ways in that situation. The commandant and Miles were both currently on my enemies list. All right, fine. I'll concede that Miles appeared to have genuinely tried to save me when the *Samaritan* snagged us. So maybe he's in the frenemy category.

"Let's circle back to this letter left by your father. You mentioned he was mad? Why would you make that accusation?" Yilmaz asked as I sat down in defeat.

"Are you kidding me? After everything that he did? Clearly, somewhere along the way, his brains got fried," I replied.

"Do the obvious mistakes in matching previous dig sites with their locations also help you come to that conclusion?"

I had seen those mistakes—glaringly obvious. Either my father had been desperate and out of time when he wrote the letter, or he didn't care if someone else could pick up on his errors.

Isoth didn't contain underground murals, nor were any waste bogs located on Mandarin's Rhine. The only planet we'd spent any significant time on that had both of those features, including sinkholes, was Epo-5. *Too obvious, Pops. Father. Whichever.*

But the reference to a silent wall of watchers and false floors didn't ring any immediate bells.

I wasn't entirely sure what to respond with, so I settled for mostly truth. "My father would never have gotten this type of information wrong. He was well-known for his attention to detail. But Epo-5 isn't anything special. As I'm sure you're aware, he took the job at Epo-5 not only to clear up the issues with conflicting work but because he'd long believed it held some kind of great galactic secret."

I hoped she already knew that last part. I remembered my father telling fantastical tales to lull my brother and me to sleep, as well as hashing out theoretical arguments with the people he worked with over the history of Epo-5. Most of them featured speculation over why a preindustrial civilization would've posed a threat to a species with technology advanced enough to travel outside their solar system.

"But in all the papers he published, he repeatedly came to the conclusions that there wasn't anything special about the planet, and the species that wiped out the indigenous population must have been looking for resources," I stated.

Minus the fact there wasn't any evidence of mining or extractions of the planet's minerals, vegetation, or other natural resources, I added to myself.

"A misdirect?" the commandant asked.

That felt like too close of a call for comfort.

"You're asking me to understand the mind of a man who went mad. Crazy. Bonkers. Cuckoo." The words rushed out as I squirmed in the chair. "If you've been keeping tabs on me—I'm upgrading you and the IGJ to stalker level now—then you know I haven't done a damned thing that would suggest I want any part of what my father was involved in."

"Perhaps," Yilmaz replied cryptically. "One last question. Have you had any recent contact with your brother, Lucas Orion?"

24

Twenty-Nine Seconds

I hadn't heard my brother's name spoken out loud in so long that hearing it was jarring. I'd only referred to him as my brother. If my father's abrupt departure and actions had stung as a betrayal, Lucas's leaving had been a relief.

Lucas and our father hadn't ever truly gotten along, not like how I'd been daddy's girl. When we were younger, sure. Lucas followed the majority of our father's ground rules and went along with almost everything. As he got older, he began to push back in ways I never did—rude comments, stolen credits, and even a few pieces of expensive tech busted up one time. Apart from all the time we'd had on our hands as kids exploring together, we'd never been particularly close.

For a long time, I thought the reason was because of our mom. I haven't talked about her much, and frankly, I don't know if I'll ever be able to.

"No," I said, finally answering the commandant's question.

The commandant nodded. "I'll escort you to the

medical bay, where you can have fifteen minutes with Mr. Turen ed-Suren. After that, my technicians will be instructed to be inventive in regards to unraveling the mysteries of your smart bots."

I paled, knowing that wasn't a threat. The woman was deadly serious.

But at least I would get my chance at getting Sam into the IGJ's system to work on the slave coding—somehow. *Okay, universe, I could really use a helping hand at this point. Hello? Universe? Are you out there?*

I didn't tumble to any great solutions as I followed the commandant into the medical bay. With no great revelations—*looking at you, universe*—I would have to make it up as I went, which didn't bode well.

The commandant ordered the medical personnel to leave the room except for one doctor and stationed the two guards at the door. *What does she think I'll do? Carry Cain out of here?*

But any other speculations over the commandant's actions flew out of my mind when I saw Cain. I wanted to rush to his side, but my body stopped, and all I could do was stare at the thin sheet covering his battered body.

"The time is ticking," the commandant whispered before she turned and left.

Wish I could shove her out an air lock.

Cain's chest barely moved up and down as I stepped next to the platform and tentatively reached out to touch his hand. I was shocked at how cold it felt.

"Is he...?" I couldn't finish the question. I'd thought he'd died once and didn't know if I could go through that emotional turmoil again.

When I didn't receive an answer, I whirled around and glared at the one doctor who'd remained. "Is he dying?"

The woman continued to stand there and stare at me, emotionless. I considered what I would do if Cain didn't make it. I would blame myself, for starters. We weren't there because of our private investigation into Project Clear Sight. That had become painfully obvious with Yilmaz's line of questioning.

The IGJ had taken us because Yilmaz was interested in the smart bots and whatever dastardly game Miles was playing out. But even though Miles shared in the culpability, ultimately, I was the one who'd agreed to play messenger. I'd agreed to a lie and a misdirect, forcing me into the arms of the Star Eaters once again.

Worse of all, if Cain died, I knew I would crawl back into my shell again and never come out. And as rapidly as our connection had grown, I was grateful for the man who'd pushed me outside of the limitations I'd placed on myself.

When I continued to stand there surrounded by silence, I huffed and stomped around to the other side of the platform and grabbed the screen.

"I would let go of that if I were you," a man told me calmly.

I looked over at the guards and noted one of them had stepped forward, one hand on his holstered weapon.

"Shoot me, for all I care," I snapped.

Well, thank goodness they must've cared a little, because they didn't shoot me, but they did spring into action. The guard who'd spoken tried to wrest the screen away from me, while his good old agent buddy grabbed at me.

When all the topsy-turvy events were mixed together and allowed to boil over, all that was left was a crazy, mixed-up soup of a woman who'd had enough.

Cain was laid out as if already dead. The whole mystery my father had left me was overwhelming, not to mention the shocker about the smart bots being tied into the horrors on the *Rapscallion*. That unhealthy stew was garnished with the aromatic herbs of being held by the IGJ. I snapped emotionally.

I was nowhere near the level of combat training IGJ agents go through, so taking them by surprise was my best bet.

I let the screen slip from my hands and forced my body to relax. The guard who had me pinned in a type of bear hug took a breath. No doubt, he was getting ready to say something pithy, but he never got the chance. Snarky comments are my domain.

I stepped wide then swung my inside leg out and behind the guard's legs. With one smooth movement, I squatted, grabbed his legs, and pulled him down. Lucky for me, his gun was holstered on the near side of his body, and I was able to draw his weapon, pivot, and shoot at the other guard.

I'd done my fair share of target practice on the range, and I was normally a decent shot in low-pressure situations. As per ChowHo Insurance policies, all passengers or employees of any spacefaring vehicle—size or purpose didn't matter—were required to take a standard weapon-safety course, along with basic emergency procedures.

Space isn't cute and cuddly, and hauling a ship full of ignorant people is a good recipe for disaster when it comes to basic safety. A lot of case law is available to read, explaining why ChowHo made it a standard policy.

But right then, with the adrenaline, fear, and a whole host of other emotions coursing through me, my aim was a whole different story.

My shot didn't hit the guard. *So much for standard-issue IGJ smart bullets.* The guard I'd taken down had scrambled to his feet and tackled me. But you can bet your shiny rockets I held on to the gun for dear life. The weapon was the only leverage I had.

The guard pinned my body to the ground and forced my arms up over my head. I rocked my hips back and forth with every ounce of strength I had and threw the guard off-balance enough that he let one of my hands go.

I slammed my palm against his ear, and the man lurched back in shock from the concussive force. Without wasting a second, I wiggled free, brought up the gun, and pulled the trigger.

All IGJ agents had access to a plethora of bioupgrades and protective tech, as my time with Cain had shown. But even against a personal shield designed to withstand close-quarter combat, several successive rounds fired nearly point-blank at the guard's chest was enough to send him sprawling to the ground in a fit of pain.

But the other guard hadn't missed a beat. I felt the heat of weapon fire as it passed by and hissed as it connected with the flooring only a few millimeters from my face.

"I've got orders not to harm you, but if you give

me a reason, I will put you down," the guard growled. "Luwa, you all right?"

The other guard nodded but had a hand up on his chest as he tried to breathe. I might've given him a broken rib or two. *Good.*

But I was out of options. Even if he had a few broken ribs, I was sure some type of repair bots or painkiller medication would be released, and the guard would be up and on his feet shortly. I surely couldn't beat the guard standing over me with his weapon held at the ready.

Evidently, I took too long to make any kind of decision, because the guard's arm swung out to the side, and he rested its muzzle against Cain's head.

"I don't, however, have any orders about not putting down the mutt."

Just for that comment alone, I was tempted to try to shoot the man before he could do anything. But I wasn't going to risk Cain's life.

Out of options, I tossed the gun. But as I did, my eyes caught sight of the screen. In the fight, it'd become dislodged from its holder and fallen to the ground. Luckily, the impact hadn't appeared to crack or damage the screen. And it wasn't that far away from me either.

Sam?

[Standing by for orders.]

I took my time as I worked to sit up. *How long will it take you to break the slave codes?*

[Conservative estimate: twenty-nine seconds.]

That might not have sounded like a long time, but twenty-nine seconds was an eternity in my situation. *You're going to have to do it in half that. On my mark.*

"You know, all I wanted was to know if Cain was dying or not," I grumbled. "The commandant did agree to me making sure he was getting the medical attention he needed."

"Fine," the guard snapped and motioned to the doctor. "Get over here."

The other guard was slowly getting to his feet, and from the pinched look on his face, the pain meds hadn't kicked in yet. That meant he was still distracted. And the guard with the gun was now distracted by the medical staff.

I rocked forward and acted as if I'd lost my balance, my hands shooting out in front of me to catch myself. I let my left hand fall on the edge of the screen.

Now.

To try to buy a few more seconds, I threw in a few hacking coughs, but unfortunately, my distress only irritated the guard, and he reached down and yanked me to my feet.

I didn't count how long my fingers had touched the screen. I should have. *Whoops.*

Did you get in?

"Doc, bring her up to speed. And make it fast. She's due for another pressing engagement," the guard ordered.

"Witty," I muttered.

The doctor went over what I was sure was only the bare minimum of Cain's medical status. I tried to pay attention, but that was hard when I was still waiting for an answer from the *Samaritan*'s AI.

Sam, did you break the slave codes?

"Mr. Turen ed-Suren has neurological degradation, massive blood loss, and appears to be in a comatose state."

"Satisfied?" the guard asked. "Now, move it."

My thoughts jumped back and forth between worrying if I'd given the AI enough time to do what it needed to do and perseverating on the words *neurological degradation* and *comatose*.

When I didn't start walking toward the door, Luwa must have begun to feel better, for he reclaimed his weapon and rammed it into my back. "He said move."

With one last look at Cain, I turned and followed their orders.

As we moved into the corridor, Sam finally responded.

[AFFIRMATIVE. WHAT ARE YOUR ORDERS, CAPTAIN?]

25

Science Experiments

Keep your systems functioning as if they're still slaved to the IGJ's system. As much as I hated my next thought, I didn't have many allies to pick from. *Can you locate Miles? And the rest of your crew?*

[Systems are being maintained at half their efficiency rating, and coding is being maintained subpar to the IGJ system. Processing orders.]

I let out a small sigh of relief. Exactly how having the *Samaritan* free of the IGJ's control was going to help, I wasn't sure. At least I had a powerful warship at my disposal. I didn't get to say something like that every day.

"What's so funny?" Luwa asked with an added shove of his weapon.

I hadn't realized I was chuckling. Perhaps that was how mad crime bosses were born. If I decided not to throw Miles out of an air lock for his little trickery with the smart bots, I might sit down and ask him.

"Nothing you would understand," I said.

"Try me," he sneered.

"Shut it. Both of you," the other guard snapped.

"Yes, sir," I replied with a mock salute.

We moved to a different deck of the ship and came to a stop in front of a narrow door.

"Janitorial closet?" I quipped. "Going to put me to work?"

"You wish," Luwa muttered.

My other guard, who rudely remained unnamed, pressed a hand against a nondescript panel beside the door. When the door opened, he stepped aside. "Ladies first."

I stepped through the door into darkness and whirled around just in time to see the door close and Luwa sending me off with a not so nice gesture.

As the door cycled shut and the telltale hum of a force field generator started up, I couldn't help but shiver.

Commandant Yilmaz's voice echoed through the dark. "Doctor 24.5.21C will be assisting us today."

What an overly dramatic theater production. I felt like I'd taken a step up in the world, compared to what Mrs. Gol had planned for me.

"What's up with the doc? Too ashamed to admit their real name?" I asked in an effort to try to direct my raising panic in another direction.

"You'll find that your father's actions precipitated the need for broader discretion," Yilmaz responded.

A light, quite dim, came to life, but unfortunately, it revealed the one thing I hadn't expected: Triton.

I gaped at the grisly scene. Yilmaz had had Mrs. Gol's unfortunate son transferred from his tube tomb on the *Rapscallion* and strung up like an animal waiting to be dissected. The thin maze of metallic tubes erupting from his body had been hooked up to some type of frame. Whatever tech had helped suspend his body in the tube wasn't at work here. His flesh had ripped and torn around the tubes from the weight of his body.

I couldn't stop the image of my own body, strung up like Triton's, from flashing through my mind, and I hadn't realized I'd been slowly backing up until I ran into the wall.

"So. That explains your line of questioning, then." I wasn't a fool, at least not all the time. "You're trying to continue what my father put a stop to. There's no way I'm letting you do that to me," I said.

Somebody new—Doctor 24.5.21C, I presumed—spoke. "If you are uncooperative, then this model of investigation may prove necessary."

When the commandant mentioned extracting the smart bots, I'd envisioned having my blood drawn multiple times. There was no way in any universe I could have dreamed up that kind of scenario.

I played the one card I had left. *Sam, take out the IGJ's weapons. Target their drive systems. Do something to throw them into a panic. Just get me out of here.*

I waited for an agonizing amount of time. I gave the commands again, screaming at the AI inside my head, but it never responded.

A dampening field. That was the only logical reason I could come up with because I couldn't handle the idea that the IGJ had figured out my connection with the *Samaritan.* I needed some thread of hope to hold on to, no matter how thin or fragile it might've been.

Another light came to life to reveal a medical platform tilted up at an angle.

A young man stepped into the light and gave me a polite smile. "Please step up onto the platform."

My eyes darted back and forth between the horrific image of Triton and the medical platform. Heart pounding, I knew I didn't have a choice. I could either resist and no doubt be manhandled or keep what little shred of dignity I had left and step onto the damned thing myself.

Tremors ran through my body as I stepped onto the foot pedestal, turned, and lay back against the cool surface of the platform.

"This may pinch, but please try to hold as still as possible," the doctor said as restraints slid across my body, encircling my wrists and ankles as the platform tilted back.

Instead of a needle or two or three moving toward my arms or neck or legs to extract my blood, with my peripheral vision, I caught sight of a pair of needles aimed directly at my head.

"Accessing temporal lobe in three… two… one… now," the doctor said as the needles pierced the sides of my head.

I arched up at the pain and screamed. Tears poured down my face as the needles punched through my skin and burrowed into my skull.

"A sedative may be necessary to prevent unwanted movement causing too much damage," the doctor said.

"No. A sedative may skew the results we're looking for. Proceed as instructed," Yilmaz countered.

"And make sure to draw another blood sample. I want our results triple-checked against the data we've been receiving."

As my vision faded, I thought of Cain. I wanted to feel his presence and have him bust down the door, the hero coming to the rescue of the damsel in distress. But the addled image I watched stepping through the door wasn't Cain. It paused, framed by the narrow rectangle of light bursting into the darkened room of horrors.

My confused mind tried to make sense of what I was seeing. I couldn't tell if the figure was a part of the light or somehow separate from the light. The image moved back and forth between those two ideas until the light filled the room and everything else was swept away.

As the space filled with a glorious blaze of warmth and illumination, I experienced the distinct sensation of weightlessness. Lazily, I moved my arms then my legs with no thought to the reality of my restraints. The light tickled, and I giggled. My worries and concerns melted away, and to my delight, I believed I could swim.

Light streamed through my fingers and flowed over my skin in a gentle caress. I closed my eyes and relished the delicious sensations pouring over me and flowing through me.

Time no longer held meaning. I could've existed in that blissful state for minutes to centuries. If the universe outside my euphoria continued to flow past me, I no longer cared.

But something encroached upon my newfound peaceful existence, just a mere hint of something that had come to unbalance and destabilize the realm where I found myself.

At first, I attempted to ignore it, wanting nothing more than to feel at ease for the rest of eternity, no longer burdened by cares or concerns. Nothing was being demanded of me, and I demanded nothing of the space I was in.

Yet the aftertaste of something sour persisted, and as it spread, I grew aware once more of the passage of time, my fears for Cain, anxieties over our situation with the IGJ, and the rage I felt at the universe for allowing all that to happen.

"The connection was established, but it appears to be weakening," someone in the distance commented.

<Cain?> I thought but remembered he was dying, laid out in a medical bay with no one there to help him. The thought sent a pulse of anger through me, and the light receded.

Half in and half out of a state of awareness, my mind struggled with wanting to ask questions. My thoughts felt as if they'd been smeared with Duteri nut butter, and everything was sticking together. But as I struggled, I did manage to free one thought: *What is this?*

I really hadn't expected to hear anything back. But surprise, surprise—sometimes, the universe does answer you.

The answers didn't come so much in a set of words but in a distorted set of impressions, as if the message had been uploaded and the data corrupted into a myriad of cascading tidbits all arranged in the wrong order. The only thing I could come away with was that something was broken, something had been lost, and everything needed to be fixed.

"First impressions?"

I knew that voice. I concentrated and worked to pull my mind free of that sticky nut butter until everything seemed to snap back into place.

Commandant Yilmaz.

The cold metal of the medical platform and its restraints stung my exposed skin, and my eyes snapped open. The room was no longer dark but well lit. Several technicians were scurrying about, and the commandant and the number doc were standing off to one side, scanning data on a large screen.

I didn't know if they realized I'd fully woken up or not, but I craned my neck to the side and read through the data myself. I didn't have a clue as to what most of it meant. In the upper left-hand corner were my vitals. From the screenshots the system had taken, I would have sworn I almost died. My heart rate, blood pressure, and brain functions had all dropped to critical levels, which was a little unnerving, to say the least.

A lot of scientific-looking data was there, with multisyllabic words I didn't have the foggiest idea how to pronounce.

"So, do I pass?" I asked.

The commandant turned and studied me.

"I do so hope I performed to your expectations and all. Do I get a shiny gold star or something?"

Yilmaz smiled, but her eyes remained cold and hard and discerning. "Your performance was adequate, well above levels in the test subjects who experienced the more… unpleasant side effects of the smart bots."

"Side effects?" I couldn't help but ask.

People say ignorance is bliss, but we were way beyond that point.

"Doctor?" the commandant asked as she deferred my question.

My numbers doc turned from the screen and in a rather bored voice rattled off medical terminology and information that made my head spin.

"Can you translate that into plain common speak?" I asked, wounding the doctor's academic sensibilities.

He scowled and threw a look the commandant's way, who nodded permission. He answered, "Malformations across the body, impaired cognition, and hallucinations."

Okay, so maybe I shouldn't have asked.

"Malformations? What in Saturn's rings are these things?"

Commandant Yilmaz cocked her head to one side. "Unstrap her," she ordered the doctor. "Then work on mimicking the modifications in the smart bots we've been able to map. I want the next round of viable candidates up and ready to go as soon as possible."

Then she turned her focus to me. "You truly don't know what's going on, do you? Your father never shared what he was working on for his entire life then abruptly decided to destroy?"

As the restraints retracted and I stepped down, a wave of dizziness washed over me. To my surprise, the commandant stuck a hand out in an offer of support.

As much as I didn't want to take it, I also didn't want to collapse in front of her or the good doctor.

"I've been trying to tell you that," I muttered.

"So it seems. Let's take a walk," she said.

26

Tea Time

The *Justus* was large, not on the scale of the *Rapscallion* or the *Samaritan* but large enough that I was hopelessly lost as I followed the commandant. As we moved through the ship with no guards, I got the sinking feeling Commandant Yilmaz's work wasn't the catch-and-release type. No one let their prisoner see that much of their ship or secret work if the captor meant them to live.

With her casual request of "Let's take a walk," I'd expected her to launch into a history lecture as we meandered through the ship. Instead, once we left the lab of doom, the commandant remained silent.

Sam? I asked the AI several times silently but never received a response. Any hope I'd harbored of using the *Samaritan* had sunk like a rock in one of Epo-5's waste bogs, sucked right down without time to say goodbye.

The commandant led me to a modest-sized commissary complete with artwork and exotic plants lending a cheerful air to the room. She took a seat and motioned for me to sit as well. I should have resisted, but I was scared, tired, and at a loss as to what to do. I sat.

When she did finally speak, I soon decided I preferred the silence.

"The worlds the InterGalactic Justice system oversee have maintained a precarious balance for several generations. I'm sure you can appreciate the difficulties in overseeing such vastly different species and cultures. More often than not, it requires a delicate touch. Subtle shifts with give-and-take scenarios to help maintain the peace. When needed, of course, the IGJ will do what is necessary, even if it means creating some rather unpleasant damage."

I really wanted to marinate in my hopelessness, but Miles's admonishment rang through my mind, and I focused on what the commandant was telling me.

"My predecessor ignored the damage caused by your father's actions for far too long. I was granted this position because the IGJ board knew I would do whatever it took in order to restore the balance and fix what had been broken." Yilmaz turned in her chair to look at me.

My stomach rolled at her gaze.

"Your father and those he worked with sought to gain power and status for humanity, an age-old story of one species trying to dominate another. But instead, they unearthed knowledge and an awareness we were never meant to have—no species was—and opened the doorway I'm now forced to walk inside with only bits and pieces of a map to guide my way," Yilmaz stated.

"By emulating them? Continuing their little science experiments?" I asked. "What do you hope to gain from all of this?"

"I had been hoping you would be able to answer that

for me. And you might still be able to, if not in words, at least through the study of those smart bots you carry." She shifted in her chair as if we were cozying up for a heart-to-heart. "Your smart bots have been modified. They're not exact replicas of the ones we've been studying from Triton's body. What we need to unravel is whether the modifications occurred because of your particular genetic makeup, or are the changes a solution to the problem?"

"Problem?" All I could envision were all the people locked away, their corpses left to rot in the *Rapscallion*. "You mean the malformations you and the good doctor were discussing."

A few of the pieces of information clicked together. "Which was why my father introduced the bacteria. To stop any further research, because it was hurting people, destroying them."

Yilmaz shrugged. "That may have been his motivation. Only he knows for sure. The bacteria killed the host, preventing the smart bots from completing their job. But I can't help but wonder if Wats did what he did because his conscience got the better of him or he simply wanted the program to go in a different direction."

I wanted to defend my father, but I couldn't. I had no idea why he did what he did or why he brought the Eeri into it all. But I knew one thing for sure. "And you're just the person for this different direction, aren't you?"

"Yes I am." Yilmaz looked confident. "Which is why you're so valuable to me at this point."

I had to stand and move around. That was way too

much information to just absorb sitting down. The commandant had told me quite a bit without actually telling me much at all.

"So, you're, what," I said as I paced back and forth, "reviving this work, trying to understand what it was my father and the others were after? If you say it was something they should never have explored, then why are you continuing their research?"

"Because there's one thing we have learned. Humanity isn't the only species that has sought this knowledge or power." She shrugged. "Or whatever it might turn out to be. All we know is that we can't let it fall into the hands of the wrong individuals. If someone is going to access this knowledge, then it's going to be us."

"Oh? And who's 'us,' the IGJ?"

"Perhaps," Yilmaz replied.

Right—factions within factions. Got it, Miles.

"So, I'm to be the start of your testing? A kick-start to picking up where good old Pops left off?"

Commandant Yilmaz laughed. "No. We've already started. We've parted with… others on the technical side of things, begun the search for the genetic coding we require. Phase one has been successfully implemented. You're helping to fill in quite a few of the blank spaces."

"You're just speaking in circles. Why don't you say something useful for a change?" I said.

"If you can provide me with something of value, then perhaps I'll return the favor," Yilmaz said with a cold smile. "I'm giving you the chance to be a part of something. To help humanity succeed and ultimately survive."

"Jump out of an air lock," I muttered. If I knew something that could've helped Yilmaz, the woman would have to pry it out of me like she was desperately trying to escape the gravitational pull of a black hole. I wasn't going to give.

"Space jumping isn't a hobby of mine," Yilmaz commented.

"Too bad," I snapped and turned to face her. "So, what now? I don't have any information for you. You going to take me back and force me to watch you butcher Cain into tiny little pieces?"

The commandant's face lost all emotion, and she fixed me with a stare that sent shivers up and down my spine. "In time. All in due time."

The conversation was over. Yilmaz stood, and I followed her as she confidently led the way back to my cell. I let my imagination run wild, thinking about all the different ways I could attack her, but I knew anything I could dream up would be useless. Anything I could do would just make her mad and probably earn a quick death for Cain.

So I focused on how we moved through the ship and tried to take note of the different decks and of anything that might be of use if I could figure out how to get free and get to Cain. Then help Cain move. And get off the *Justus* without alerting anyone. Then make it over to the *Samaritan*. Too many *and*s and *then*s.

Defeated and overwhelmed, I stepped into my cell without fussing. I heard the zap and steady hum of the force field and lay down on the unforgiving slab they deemed worthy enough to be a bed.

I rolled over and curled up into a ball, trying to keep the image of Cain's bloody tail out of my mind.

Sam?

[CONNECTION HAS BEEN REESTABLISHED. DO YOU WISH TO PROCEED?]

Holy Jupiter, yes I wish to proceed! Where were you?

[CONNECTION WAS LOST DUE TO A SHIELDING FIELD. CONNECTION WAS REESTABLISHED BUT DETECTED AN INTERPRETER FIELD.]

Interpreter field? That's a new one on me.

[AN INTERPRETER FIELD IS A WIDE-RANGE BROADCASTING TRACKING SIGNAL. FIRST DESIGNED BY A MASTER GLIPGLOW ON—]

That's okay. I don't need a history lesson right now.

[COMMANDS, CAPTAIN?]

Are you still flying under the IGJ radar, so to speak?

[PLEASE REPHRASE THE COMMAND.]

You're going to have to update your language banks.

[A LANGUAGE UPDATE WILL REQUIRE A SYSTEM HOOK INTO A MAIN-LANGUAGE DATABASE. PLEASE STATE THE—]

I was kidding. Well, not really. But that's not a command for right now. Sam, are you still maintaining a false slave reading to the IGJ system?

[YES.]

I wanted to laugh, cry, and scream all at the same time.

Sam. I had a new thought. *Can you break into the ship's medical records? Can you give me updates on how Cain is doing?*

[ONE MOMENT.]

I waited, my anxiety growing. Being able to know how Cain was doing wouldn't help me free him, but it would at least give me a little peace of mind. Even if the news was bad, I needed to know.

[CONNECTION ESTABLISHED. I CAN MAINTAIN A FIFTEEN-SECOND SCAN BURST BEFORE DETECTION. THERE IS NO CAIN LISTED ON THE MEDICAL LISTS.]

Oh, right. Turen ed-Suren.

[TUREN ED-SUREN. HIS CONDITION IS STABLE. CURRENTLY KEPT SEDATED. HEART RATE IS WITHIN NORMAL PARAMETERS. BLOOD PRESSURE ISN'T OPTIMAL BUT WITHIN ACCEPTABLE LEVELS. CAPTAIN, I DETECT YOU HAVE NO BIOHARDWARE FOR OCULAR IMPLANTS, BUT I CAN ACTIVATE AN AUDITORY SUBROUTINE TO PROVIDE AUTOMATIC INFORMATIONAL UPDATES FOR PERSONNEL.]

That sounded like a great idea, and relief washed over me at hearing Cain was stable. That meant we were still within the window of time before the nanobots were activated.

Sam, do it. Initiate that subroutine protocol. Provide automatic updates for Turen ed-Suren and Miles High. I might not like the guy, but keeping tabs on him also would be good.

[COMMAND INITIATED. FURTHER INSTRUCTIONS?]

I didn't know. Maybe Sam could blow a hole in the side of the ship. But that wouldn't have done me any good.

Stand by. I needed to think. Some food wouldn't hurt either. But I doubted the *Justus* had a menu I could order from.

27

Reunions… Oh, So Much Fun

I didn't know when I drifted off to sleep, only that I was woken up by a sharp slap to the face.

"Get up," a woman hissed.

I sat up and rubbed my eyes, surprised at how well rested I felt. Apparently, being interrogated, seeing someone you cared about threatened, and being told you're infected with a nefarious science experiment your father was mixed up in could help someone sleep like the dead.

Once I was up, the guard jerked a thumb toward the door. "Get moving."

"Where are you taking me?"

"Shut it and follow orders," she snapped.

All right, not the I'll-put-a-mint-on-your-pillow-for-you type of guard.

We walked down the hallway with enough twists and turns that I lost my bearings until we came to another nondescript door with a guard on either side.

"Open it up," the woman ordered.

The man on the right snapped to attention, turned,

and punched in a code. The door slid open to reveal a larger room, well lit and filled with people.

"Oh, party time," I commented.

"Smart-ass," the woman said as she shoved me through the door.

It slid shut behind me. All eyes turned to stare at me. I stared back.

Then Sam began to speak: [*Flight deck attendant Shiro. All biosigns read normal. Bioupgrades temporarily disabled. Mechanic subclass two Pip Harrington. All biosigns read normal. Bioupgrades temporarily disabled. Weapons specialist Eto. Broken rib. Swelling of his right eye with hairline fractures in the orbital bone. Bioupgrades temporarily disabled.*]

Sam went through a dozen more names and statuses before I realized what she was doing. I'd ordered the subroutine, but I hadn't expected that. I'd figured my order had only initiated updates for Cain and Miles, but as my brain caught up with what Sam was reporting, I realized that would've been a nifty ocular feature for the captain, an easy way to identify crew on a large vessel that housed over five hundred crew members plus additional combatant personnel.

I swung my head back and forth, taking in who was left until Sam stopped on the one person I did know.

[*Zhu Akio. Two broken ribs. Fractured tibia in the left arm. Hairline fractures found in metacarpal bones in both hands. Dislocated left shoulder. Bioupgrades temporarily disabled.*]

I did hear Sam, but at that moment, all I thought about was everything was Miles's fault. A little thundercloud of anger sprang to life inside me, and I lunged for the man.

"What have you done?" I snarled as I leaped forward and found my fingers closing around Miles's neck.

Not even trying to resist, Miles stood there and took my abuse. No one made a move to try to stop me either. I hadn't expected that, and when he didn't fight back, my burst of rage turned into a bout of annoyance.

"What's going on?" I asked as my hands slipped away from his neck. I was at least satisfied with the red marks I'd left, a small price to pay for what I knew he'd done.

Miles gave me a defeated look. His facial skin sagged as if the man had aged several years in the short time we'd been in IGJ custody. His eyes were bloodshot, and his eyelids drooped. I half wondered if he was going to fall asleep on me.

"Are you drugged?" I asked and took a step closer. *Sam, is he drugged?*

[Hold, please.]

I watched him as I waited for Sam to respond. I wouldn't have put it past Yilmaz to resort to all sorts of underhanded interrogation techniques to glean the information she was searching for.

[Records show a nonnarcotic drug administered for pain relief. Last dosage was four hours. No other recorded drugs have been authorized for Zhu Akio.]

"So that's a no, then," I muttered and waved a hand in front of his face. "At least on record. Doesn't mean Yilmaz wouldn't work off the books." I considered the infuriating man standing in front of me. *What do I do now?*

But Miles had been studying me in turn, and I saw a flash of understanding in his eyes.

"You foolish chit," he hissed. He reached out and pulled me down with him to sit on a bench. With his lips barely moving, in an annoying whisper, he asked, "You're hooked in?"

At least I was able to read between the lines that time. I nodded. "How did you know?"

"The *Samaritan* is my ship. I know what she's capable of," he hissed. "But this doesn't matter. The less we say, the better. Understand?"

I nodded.

"Cain?" he asked.

I couldn't quite let go of the anger I felt toward Miles. "Why do you care?"

Miles leaned back and didn't try to mask his words. "Despite events of late, I do care what happens to the buffoon. He knows a lot of valuable information"—he twisted in his seat and stared up at what I could only presume was a camera—"which I keep trying to tell these lug heads. Cain isn't disposable… or a tool to be used. They kill him, and they lose a valuable piece of the puzzle."

"You've got to be kidding. You're the one who stuffed him full of the exploding death bots. Now you're saying he's valuable?"

"What I'm interested in, they're interested in."

I raised an eyebrow. "Really?"

Miles stared at me, and I abruptly felt the fool. He was actually trying to keep Cain alive, trying to make the IGJ believe he really did need him.

The realization must have shown on my face because Miles shook his head with a frown. "If you're going to survive what's coming, you're going to have to become a better poker player than this. Didn't your father teach you anything?"

I scowled. "I'm getting awfully tired of you making that type of comment. What's done is done. Time to move forward." I paused then muttered, "If there is a way to move forward."

I could feel Miles studying me but didn't care. Instead, I turned in my seat to gaze at the others in the room. "Is this all that's left? What about Dr. Ashter?"

"I don't know. They won't say, of course," Miles replied and, with a bit of distaste, added, "But I'm sure the good doctor will find a way to survive. He always does."

After a contemplative silence, I turned back to face him. He was still watching me.

"I'm assuming they threw me in here to see what we would do," I said.

"Good. Some of those smarts showing up again," Miles said. "And I'm assuming that meant you haven't told them much."

I shook my head, and for some odd reason, I couldn't stop the tears that welled up. "I should have," I whispered.

"Whatever they've done, it was bound to happen in one form or another. They're getting desperate. I'm not sure why."

"She had his tail cut off," I mumbled through the tears.

Miles's eyes widened as genuine shock, grief, and anger appeared on his face. "They did what?"

But I couldn't repeat it. Just mentioning it brought the image back to the forefront of my mind, and I couldn't shake it.

"He's barely holding on. I got to go in and see him. But I don't know if… if he'll…" I couldn't say it.

For a brief moment, all the masks Miles wore slipped away, and Akio sat before me. He reached out and took my hands in his and brought them up to his lips. After a gentle kiss on the back of each hand, he brought them up to touch his forehead.

I recognized the gesture and was shocked. "But you hate him."

Miles lowered my hands and stared at me. "I don't hate him. We are simply reminders to the other of what we've sacrificed and lost."

"I don't understand," I said.

With a long sigh, Miles released my hands and leaned back. "You know who Cain is?"

I nodded. "The son of Chancellor Heron, who oversees the Aligned Worlds."

"Correct. Cookie for the lady. As you can imagine, the chancellor moves in the same circles as the monarchs of Old Earth," Miles said and waited until he saw the pieces begin to connect.

I wondered why I hadn't tumbled to it before. "You knew each other growing up, didn't you?"

"Cookie number two," Miles said with a rueful grin. "We did."

"So what happened?" I asked.

Miles shook his head. "That is for Cain to say. Not I."

I frowned, frustrated at getting a small piece of the Cain puzzle then having the information stop when it was getting good.

"Right now, we have much bigger poli-fish to fry," Miles said.

He was right. Cain's story wouldn't mean as much to me if he didn't survive his ordeal. I didn't know if I could bear learning any more about him if I knew I would never get to be with him again.

I gave myself a bit of a mental shake. If I wanted Cain to live, I needed to get my butt in gear. I let the anger creep back into my voice. "Right, but when we're out of this mess, you owe me an explanation about the setup in the neutral zone."

That wasn't a question or a request. Miles had a lot of explaining to do.

He nodded. "My word."

"Fine. Now, to clarify. If there was no message, what about the deadline you set? More fun and games? We've got to be close to the cutoff for his nanobots."

"Unfortunately, we're past the mark."

I sat up a little straighter. "What?" *Sam, what's the time and date? Old Earth standard.* I didn't know why I hadn't I asked earlier. *Because you're letting your emotions fuel your actions. Get it together. Be logical and focused.*

[OLD EARTH STANDARD. CONVENTIONAL CALENDAR. 2622.11.9.]

"My best guess is we're at least twenty-four hours past it," Miles said.

"Wrong," I whispered, relief flooding me. "We're two days past your deadline. But Cain's still alive."

"And you know this for sure?"

I nodded. "Yes. I've seen him."

He leaned back. "Good. The bots weren't anything special and would have shown up on the IGJ's scans. At least they had the decency to remove them."

"Decency?" I growled. "Only so they could keep him alive and torture him. To try and get to me."

Miles at least had the good grace to look ashamed, as well he should. I was learning Miles thrived on chaos, but putting a ticking time bomb into someone was a whole other level of crazy. The implications were grotesque. *If Cain had been around a group of people or a vulnerable piece of vital tech…* I shuddered just thinking about it.

I grinned. "How much of a punch do those suckers make?"

Miles narrowed his eyes and considered my question. "Enough to cause internal damage and put the ship in emergency mode. Why?"

"Leave it to me. Just be ready," I said.

I wasn't sure Miles had much confidence in me, but he nodded and accepted the order anyway. Yilmaz had been too desperate for information, hoping that I'd been an expert liar or that Miles would slip up when he saw me. But putting us together to observe how we interacted was going to be her downfall.

I was going to free Cain and get off that blasted ship.

28

The Death Hook Advantage

Miles changed the conversation to misdirects and inane topics. I had no doubt that whoever was watching and listening boiled over, because an extremely grumpy woman stormed into the room, pulled me to my feet, and shoved me into the hallway.

Sam? Can you give me info on the IGJ *personnel too?* I asked, praying that no more interceptor fields would prevent Sam from communicating with me.

Thankfully, nothing did.

[AFFIRMATIVE.]

*[*IGJ *AGENT FIRST CLASS ANNABELLE LUKOWSKI. BIO-SIGNS NORMAL. BIOUPGRADES IN OPERATION. WOULD YOU LIKE THOSE LISTED?]*

No.

I had no idea what I would do with the information, but maybe I could remember their names and faces and make them pay for what they'd done. Besides, knowing who they were took away some of the scary factors as I was led through the ship. They might've been on the wrong side—which, of course, meant they weren't on my side—but they were still individuals going through their lives and following orders.

"Where are you taking me? I demand to see Cain. I need to see if you've given him the medical help he needs." I bombarded the surly woman with questions until she had enough.

"Shut it, Orion. You're in no position to make demands. Besides, I've already got orders to take you to medical. So you're in luck."

I couldn't have asked for an easier setup if I'd gotten down and begged on my knees and coughed up everything I knew. That put me on edge. I'd prepared a whole gamut of annoying speeches to worm my way back into medical.

When I was unceremoniously shoved into the room, Yilmaz was standing on the far side of Cain's medical platform. My earlier statement about an easy setup was probably incorrect. No doubt, Yilmaz wasn't up to anything cozy.

[Turen ed-Suren. Condition unchanged since last update. Commandant Hazine Umtholopali Yilmaz of the InterGalactic Justice system. Biosigns normal. Bioupgrades in operation. Doctor Karin Ern. General medic with an eight-star rating and clearance for midlevel classified intel. Biosigns normal. Bioupgrades in operation. Doctors Assistant Level Two Surrena Smith. Biosigns—]

That's good, Sam. Thanks.

"Last chance, Ms. Mahia," Yilmaz said. "I would appreciate an update after your time with Zhu Akio. If not, I'm afraid Mr. Turen ed-Suren won't be making it.

But don't fret—I'll see to it that he's given a hero's-death award. It will at least placate his mother."

I clenched my jaw and balled my hands into fists at the commandant's casual dismissal of Cain. "Miles deserves some air lock time, but that's about all there is."

Yilmaz gave me a thoughtful look then motioned to the doctor. "Doctor Ern, if you please."

"So polite during this whole messy business, aren't you," I said. "You must've threatened and killed a heap of individuals over the years to be as comfortable with all of this as you are."

The commandant laughed at me. "My poor child, you don't know even half of what I've had to do in order to be in this position." Her demeanor changed like someone had flipped a switch. "But I can assure you"—her eyes gleamed with malice—"I earned this position because I've got a proven track record of doing exactly what it takes in order to see results."

"At your command," Doctor Ern said.

The woman turned toward me with a blank look on her face. Her hand was hovering just above Cain's neck, and I recognized she was holding a miniature death hook with a glowing red light indicating it was active.

I'd never seen one in action in person, only on the media. Death hooks were human tech designed in the early years of human exploration into space. The hook was meant to provide a painless and instantaneous death.

Those weren't covered in most schools. The practice was originally kept hush-hush by the mining corporations that funded their development. Accidents were commonplace during asteroid mining work before AI interfaces and robotics refined the process and allowed humans to work in much safer environments.

Those early mining corporations operated on thin budgets and didn't waste money on expensive medical gear or personnel. Cutting their losses was much easier by fabricating stories of unfortunate accidents when, in reality, they didn't want to shell out medical expenses for employees who'd been seriously injured during the line of duty.

When someone was injured beyond the effectiveness of what horribly little medical treatment they could receive, the death hook was deployed. The employee died, and the company scavenged what equipment or gear they could then tossed the body out an air lock.

The whole venture became so horrid that at the Inver Mining Fields, people had to maneuver around more dead bodies than asteroids. *Pretty grim, I know.* I was glad I didn't grow up in those times. Also, imagine the type of people the mining corporations employed who were able to work in that kind of environment. The commandant would have been right at home.

"I can assure you, your fate will be far worse than his," Yilmaz said, breaking into my little internal history monologue. "Triton can always use more company."

I paled at her promise. It wasn't a threat. The woman was crazy. Sane-crazy. Far more dangerous than Mrs. Gol had been.

I wondered if I could get out of the situation alive.

The odds weren't in my favor. But I had to try, and I needed to stall. I let my shoulders slump forward and hung my head. The tears weren't hard to fake.

Sam. Where are the nanobots the IGJ *removed from Cain's body?*

[TWO DECKS BELOW YOUR PRESENT LOCATION.]

Next was the thousand-credit question. *Can you activate them?*

[YES.]

Praise anything and everything. Thank Jupiter and Saturn's rings. Bless Pluto and its identity crisis.

What's the blast radius? And estimated damage?

[THE NANOBOTS ARE THREE METERS FROM AN OUTER HULL WALL. IF THE BLASTING MATRIX HASN'T BEEN COMPROMISED BY COLD STORAGE, THE BLAST WILL CREATE A METER-WIDE HOLE IN THE HULL. ALL PERSONNEL WITHIN THE ROOM HAVE A TWENTY-PERCENT SURVIVAL RATE. IGJ SYSTEM RESPONSE TIME IS UNDER TEN SECONDS BEFORE TEMPORARY SHIELDING WILL BE ACTIVATED.]

But in the meantime, they won't know what hit them. Sam, you've got nine seconds to break off from the IGJ *ship. When you do, target weapons and life-support systems. Oh, and bring down all security locks.*

[ON YOUR COMMAND.]

I looked up at Yilmaz and saw a flash of triumph. *Pride cometh before the fall*, I thought to myself.

"If you think I'm going to be strung up like Triton, you've got another thing coming," I said.

Now.

We didn't hear the blast and felt only a small vibration through the flooring. But the ship's emergency system kicked into action, and the lights switched to the standard red glow to indicate an emergency.

Yilmaz snapped into action as I figured she would. The woman raced over to one of the larger screens and entered a series of codes.

"Captain, report," the commandant ordered.

As Yilmaz listened to the captain's update, she turned and snapped her fingers at the doctor.

"Oh no you don't," I muttered and leaped over the table to crash into the doctor. We tumbled to the floor in a tangled mass of limbs, but it wasn't that much of a struggle. Either Doctor Ern had never received much hand-to-hand combat training, or she just wasn't very committed to Yilmaz and the IGJ.

In a matter of seconds, I wrested the death hook away from her, and the doctor scrambled away and pleaded for her life.

I threw her a disgusted look. "Get out of here," I snarled.

The doctor's panicked expression sagged in relief then morphed into a blank expression. Knowing what that meant, I ducked and rolled to one side just in time to avoid the commandant's kick. I jumped to my feet but received a hearty punch to my side. Pain exploded through my abdomen, and I fell to my knees. Reeling from the pain, I swung wide with the death hook and missed Yilmaz's leg by only a few millimeters. Forcing the commandant to jump back at least gave me the few seconds I needed to get back to my feet. Physically, I wasn't capable of winning a fight with the woman, but I had the advantage with the death hook.

The ship took an opportunity to give a massive shudder, and we both lost our balance. Yilmaz recovered first and began yelling orders.

At least no one had seen fit to strip me of my maglock boots. I turned them on and braced for the next round of fire.

The pain was still in my side but dissipating, and I had to renege on my offer of freedom to the doctor. She'd gotten to her feet and was clutching an empty medical platform for support.

I took a menacing step forward and brandished the death hook. "Wake him up. Now."

The doctor's eyes moved from my face to the death hook and over to where Yilmaz was giving orders to her agents through the screens.

I leaned forward, not fooling around anymore. "Do it, or you're dead."

Thankfully, the doctor believed me because unfortunately, I believed myself. But I would have to spend time psychoanalyzing myself later. *If we live through any of this.*

"Secure the prisoner!" Yilmaz shouted and laughed at my moment of trying to help Cain.

I spun around as Yilmaz waved a dismissive hand at two agents who had entered the room.

Sam was excellent at multitasking. *[Agent Usa Kilo. Biosigns normal. Bioupgrades in operation. Agent Ted Zurick. Biosigns normal. Bioupgrades in operation.]*

Yilmaz stopped issuing orders and turned to give me a tight smile. "I'll be seeing you."

"Not without a reservation," I replied.

The two agents didn't waste time, and neither did I.

While the doctor was working to revive Cain—I guess she wanted to hedge her bets in case I won—I needed to figure out a way to survive the two agents approaching with their weapons drawn. So I used the only leverage I had.

I moved to stand behind the doctor and held the death hook at her neck.

"Your ship's a tad bit unsteady at the moment," I said. "You guys come any closer, and the next blast might accidentally cause me to kill her."

They hesitated but only for a moment. *Blast it all out of an air lock.* I'd hoped for more compassion than that.

"Come on, guys. You don't want to lose a doc, do you?"

Evidently, they did.

Sam, I could use a little help here. A distraction or something.

[HOLD, PLEASE.]

Okay, I thought, suddenly learning how insufferably annoying that was. *Talk about some instakarma.*

[TACTICAL BURST IN THREE… TWO… ONE.]

I lowered my hand away from the doc and braced, which the agents took as a sign of surrender. When the ship abruptly rocked side to side, I was highly disappointed to see the efficiency of my opponents, who'd already switched on their mag-lock boots. At least they were thrown off-balance and weren't able to line up a great shot.

Sam, get Miles and someone else up here to help.

I'm not above asking for help when I need it. Besides, I couldn't carry Cain out of there on my own. The doctor had succeeded in reviving him, but in his current state, he wasn't stable enough to move through a ship in the midst of a battle on his own. I would need Miles and the rest of the crew to help get him out of there. But having them coming didn't solve the immediate problem, the two agents.

It was all or nothing. I shoved the doctor to one side, and she scrambled over to hide in a corner. I'd expected more from someone under IGJ employment. But I wasn't complaining, since her self-preservation helped me out.

I really wished I'd had Cain's personnel shielding. But all I had to do was stall, keeping them occupied long enough that Miles and the others could arrive to help.

So I did the one thing I knew how to do.

"Do you two carry any Confore technology on you? In you? Or about you?" I asked.

The two guards shared a quick look.

"I'll just assume you do. A couple of years ago, Confore released an integrated olfactory enhancement nodule. Not the best piece of work, let me tell you." I raised my hands and stepped to the end of the medical platform. From the corner of my eye, I saw Cain's head shift and one eyelid slowly open.

"There are only a couple of species that appreciate the full spectrum of olfactory senses. Most species, humans included, enjoy what we can but are quite content with not being able to smell every little thing. Like a piece of rotting food from over ten meters away. Or a Neetho long-haul freighter. Have you ever stepped into one of those? I'm telling you, it's best to stay away."

I took a step forward.

"You'll surrender your weapon and come with us," Usa ordered.

"Sorry, no can do at the moment," I replied.

"Surrender the weapon, or we shoot," Ted threatened.

"Sheesh, fine, okay, just hang on a sec," I said. Slowly, I bent over, praying with every millimeter as I lowered the weapon that Miles or someone on my side would burst through the door.

I'd been looking in the wrong direction.

Shock registered on both of the agents' faces as Cain rolled himself off the platform, took only a second to orient himself, then leaped at the two agents with a primal roar of defiance I'll never forget.

As he moved through the air, he flung his arms wide and knocked both of the agents off their feet.

Without thinking, I rushed forward and kicked at Usa as she was already rolling toward Cain. I bent down and pierced her skin with the death hook. Within a second, her body went rigid then slack.

What I'd done didn't register until much later. At that moment, I was focused on protecting Cain, and my actions had leveled the playing field. Cain got the upper hand with Ted, took his gun, and at point-blank range, shot the man.

Cain looked up at me, his irises coal black and blood trickling down his chin. I couldn't help but stare in horror as I realized he'd not only turned Ted's weapon inward and fired, he'd bitten the man's neck as well.

Now that the threat was contained, the energy drained from Cain's body, and he toppled to the floor between the dead agents. Deactivating the death hook, I dropped it into one of my jumpsuit pockets and rushed over to Cain. I fell to my knees and shook him. Looking up, I noted the doctor was still crouched down in the corner.

"Do something!" I shouted.

But neither one of them moved.

I cradled Cain's head in my lap and ran my fingers lightly down the side of his face. His eyes fluttered open, and the black was fading to a dusty amber.

<I'm sorry,> he sent.

"You've got nothing to be sorry for," I said as I brushed his hair out of his face. "You're my heart's blood."

He relaxed against my touch, and when I pulled back, his eyes were closed. I pulled him closer to my body and rocked back and forth.

But the moment was spoiled when I heard the door open. With a vicious snarl, I twisted to see who it was.

But it was only Miles. He stepped into the medical bay, took one look, and began issuing orders.

"You're too late," I whispered against Cain's skin. "You're too late."

29

Word Puzzles

"Mahia, I need you to focus!" Miles was shouting at me. "Mahia!"

I looked up through tearstained eyes. "Why? He's dead."

"Good night, woman, get a hold of yourself. He's not dead. We'll sedate him and get him out of here. I've sent my group to secure a shuttle bay, but we can't waste any more time," Miles snapped.

"Not dead?" I asked, feeling like I'd been sitting on the med bay's floor for an eternity.

Members of Miles's crew gently took Cain from me and transferred him to a mobile medical platform.

Miles crouched down next to me. "He'll survive. He's tough. But we've got to get off this ship." He reached out and squeezed my shoulder. "I made you a promise, and I intend to keep it. But I need you to do your part."

With a shuddering breath, I fought to regain control and focused on Cain as I pushed myself to my feet. "What do you need?"

"That's my girl," Miles said with a grin. "We're pinned

down in four different groups. Whatever you and Sam did was enough to distract the IGJ and get us all loose but not enough to incapacitate the *Justus*. We need Sam to help secure routes so we can all head to the shuttle bay. Pronto."

Sam? Can you help everyone make it to the shuttle bay? Maybe rolling lockouts throughout the decks and sections to keep the IGJ *guessing for a few minutes as to where we're headed?*

*[*Hold, please.*]*

If you're going to do that, you should play some music.

*[*Unable to process. Please restate the command.*]*

We need the Justus *to have some type of rolling lockouts—*

*[*Those commands are being implemented. Please restate your most recent command.*]*

Oh, never mind. Thanks.

I would've thought that a warship AI would understand a few more colloquial phrases.

"Sam's got it," I said.

"Good," Miles said with a determined grin. "Stick close and follow us."

Miles didn't have to tell me twice. I walked behind one of the two crewmen transporting Cain and reached out to lightly touch Cain's shoulder.

<We'll get through this.>

I wanted to believe I felt something of his presence, but maybe I just needed to be reassured and convinced myself that Cain was truly trying to respond to my touch and thoughts.

Sam was good, better even than I was expecting, based on my commands. We moved through the *Justus* with little resistance. Bulkheads locked and unlocked before and after us, guiding us toward the shuttle bay. A few IGJ agents slipped through the doors before they closed, but Miles proved a far deadlier adversary than I would've pegged him for. Oh, I knew he could fight after our little tussle on the *Whimsy*, but I hadn't taken him for an expert marksman. I should have known.

Sam, how far out are we?

[Take the next right, travel three meters, and turn left. Follow the corridor to the end then move up a deck. The shuttle bay will be on your right.]

We were almost there, almost to safety. I reached out and touched Cain's shoulder to comfort myself. *<Just a little more, then we'll be able to board the* Samaritan *and get the hell out of IGJ adventure land.>*

Miles moved into the next section, checking the intersection. When he gave the all clear, the crewmen guiding the mobile platform stepped over the bulkhead's lip in the floor. Right then, I felt a sting then a burn as it radiated across my back. As I fell to my knees, Miles whipped around and raised his weapon to fire. I didn't have to turn around to know who'd fired the shot.

Sam, seal the door. Now!

I looked up at Miles as the bulkhead closed. "You made a promise. Now keep it."

Hesitation showed on his face as his eyes flickered to where the control panel should be.

"Go!" I hollered at him as the door sealed shut.

Sam, seal the bulkhead behind us. Monitor these two bulkheads. Rotate the codes. I need them sealed until I tell you otherwise.

[Affirmative.]

"If you're going to kill me, get it over with, already," I said as a pair of boots walked past me.

"You may not be as knowledgeable as I'd hoped, but you're still of use to me. You'll have to wait for a while before I grant you that mercy," Yilmaz said.

I don't think you're going to get the chance.

Yilmaz had hit me with a stunner, a nasty piece of tech designed to paralyze the extremities—with a fair amount of pain—for ninety seconds. I was able, at least, to look up at Yilmaz.

[Commandant Hazine Umtholopali Yilmaz of the InterGalactic Justice—]

That's good, Sam. I've got it. I don't need to hear her name again or—

Wait. Her name. Her middle name. I'd been too concerned about Cain to make the connection when I heard the commandant's full name the first time.

[Please restate command.]

I'm good, Sam. I don't need the names of everyone right now.

[Acknowledged.]

Yilmaz wasn't even attempting to keep her enjoyment hidden this time as she stared at me. She did have a sadistic streak.

"So you're… what? Going to string me up like Triton? Open me up piece by piece until you understand what makes those smart bots tick? Is that the plan?"

Yilmaz snorted. "You are woefully ignorant, aren't you. One would think growing up under the tutelage of Wats Hawking Orion, being able to travel the known worlds and a few of the ones lost to history, would have created a more well-rounded and knowledgeable woman. More's the pity."

"Yeah? You think I'm not well-rounded? What makes you so much more rotund than me?"

Yilmaz crouched down. "My father was a traveling diplomat. Contracted out to various worlds. I was born on—"

"Wait. Let me guess. The Lesser Seeds of Irolo? The place must have made a big impression on your parents. And you say your father was a diplomat. Interesting."

For once, Yilmaz looked surprised. "My parents had been stationed there for thirteen years before my birth." Her guard went up, and she narrowed her eyes. "Why?"

"Oh, nothing. I know how it's commonplace for diplomats to name their kids after important cultural references where they're stationed. Seems to gain political favor in a lot of species. And your middle name is interesting. Wouldn't peg it as a common choice for humans… unless you've got some Irolo ancestry in there somewhere?"

Finally, I'd caught the commandant off guard, so I continued. "Your middle name is Umtholopali, which means 'an endless or ceaseless horizon.'" And as I said those words, I knew where I'd recognized that piece of artwork from. "And that fine piece of art in your office? That's an artistic rendering of the Opali Yil Nebula? Right?"

I felt a distinct tingle in my arms and legs as the effects of the stunner wore off.

"See, I've learned plenty. Languages and culture and politics. Being able to find bits and pieces of information and put it together." And because I felt the need to prove a point, I responded in Irolo.

Yilmaz smirked. "A neat party trick. But it still doesn't tell me you've actually learned anything useful."

I snorted. "Of course I have. I might not know what motivated my father, but you were behind the Opali-Poli company, weren't you? What was it, a touch of arrogance or pride? Wait, was it nostalgia over the Lesser Seeds? No matter, though. And I'm also betting you had something to do with Jorge. He would have had access to your profile and connected the dots too."

Yilmaz frowned, and I knew it was now or never. The tingling was fading, and that was my chance. I threw myself against the commandant, and she lost her balance and toppled backward. Before she had a chance to react, I was on top of her, and I pulled the death hook out of my pocket.

Yilmaz tensed, but when I held the death hook up and twisted it back and forth to let her get a good look, she went slack.

"What I don't get, though, is what the SeeClear updates have to do with your little quest concerning the smart bots. What did Jorge find, which made him a threat… and sent the Weplies off the deep end, thinking I was a part of it all?"

To her credit, Yilmaz didn't bat an eye or try to whine or plead but kept right on glaring. If not for the death hook at her neck, I know the woman would've killed me on the spot, from the look in her eyes. But she didn't have a death wish and stayed still.

"Tell me, or the IGJ begins interviews for a new commandant."

"You wouldn't dare," she hissed.

"Try me." At that moment, I meant it, just as I had with the doctor.

The woman had authorized the brutality against Cain and wasn't above using me as some type of lab rat. The worlds really wouldn't be worse off without her.

<They probably wouldn't. But you aren't that person.>

<Cain?>

<I'm here. I'm with you,> he replied.

I could've wept buckets of tears at hearing his voice rattling around inside my skull.

<Then you're safe?> I asked.

<Not until you're here with me.>

Thankfully, Yilmaz believed my threat and decided a few answers might score her a few brownie points.

"Agent Jorge opened up a case file he dubbed Project Clear Sight. He was a good agent and, at first, believed there was some kind of connection to a disruption in the stock market and false credit streams. He petitioned for the case to be sent off to the Jumjul. But I dismissed the case and shut it down. Sadly, Jorge was a very determined agent."

I narrowed my eyes and thought furiously. "Which is why you must have, what, tried to bury the case?"

"Yes. But Jorge was stubborn and went around his section leader to conduct an undercover investigation. Unfortunately for him, he figured out what was behind the SeeClear 3.5 upgrade," Yilmaz replied. "And the

Weplies… Well, they have a tendency to overreact when it comes to potential Jumjul intervention.”

The upgrade. The lines at Lunar 5 waiting to receive the software. I tried to recall what she'd said earlier. *Something about phase one already being initiated and technological solutions in reference to… Come on. Think, Mahia.*

Solutions to finding genetic matches.

“The software hacks into the HalfLife biochips, doesn't it?” I asked. “It's the perfect back door into a treasure trove of medical data.”

Yilmaz smiled. “All the medical records and genetic profiles we could ask for.”

“Which fly in the face of the accords set down with the Jumjul High Court. Not to mention half a dozen worlds and their strict laws regarding the use of HalfLife data. So my lovely former bosses needed to make sure any potential blowback was taken care of, right? That included me because, being human, I might have been Jorge's sidekick or confidant,” I said. “But why not go through proper channels? You're researching humanity, not the entirety of the known worlds. You've got the authority.”

“And trigger alerts? Your father might have stopped the bulk of the work his group had done, but his actions didn't put a stop to all the research. I'm not the only one out there looking for the necessary components to get the answers.”

“Well, you're not going to—” I stopped. Everything I knew so far clicked into place.

Mrs. Gol. Poor, crazy Mrs. Gol had talked about generations of selective breeding. I thought she even said my father had been the best of them at one point. They had bred themselves and their sons and daughters in the hopes of creating some perfect human specimen, and Yilmaz was looking for those ideal candidates, using the SeeClear 3.5 tech.

I leaned back as my head swam due to all that information. Yilmaz took the opening and tried to gain the upper hand. Her sudden movement startled me, and before I could correct myself, the death hook snagged the inside of her jacket collar. The instant the material touched her skin, Yilmaz began to foam at the mouth, and her body twitched. I scrambled off her and stared. If Yilmaz had been anyone else, she surely would have died in time, but as the commandant of the IGJ, whatever bioupgrades she sported went to work but not before some serious physiological effects were going to take place.

The puzzle of Project Clear Sight had been solved.

Another shudder ran through the *Justus*, and I mentally gave myself a kick in the rear, realizing I was wasting time.

Sam, open the doors and get me out of here.

I got up, turned, and ran.

30

The Lines Are Drawn

Getting off the *Justus* turned out to be easier than expected. Sam had maintained control of the systems long enough to get me to the shuttle bay without a hitch. Two of the *Samaritan*'s crew were there, waiting for me. Once we docked with our ship, I ran through the corridors to check up on Cain. Instead, I slammed into Miles.

"You're needed on the bridge, Captain," he said.

I didn't think he was very happy about my new job title.

"No. I'm going to see Cain," I said, trying to shove my way past him.

"And I want to survive this. But the *Samaritan* needs its captain focused and informed," Miles snapped.

"You can be the captain. I don't want it. What in all that's holy do you think I know about being a captain?"

"Then you should have thought twice before eating a piece of tech you didn't know anything about," Miles retorted.

Touché. "Well, I don't give a—"

Miles slapped me. So I punched him back.

"Get it together, Orion. If we don't make it out of here, Cain doesn't live. Got it?" he snapped.

Fine. But I thought I was due a bit of grace for my actions, considering everything that'd happened. Angry, annoyed, and very much frightened, I let Miles guide me up to command.

"Is he at least okay? How is he doing?" I couldn't help but ask.

Miles was more than irritated. "Cain will survive as long as you do your part."

I considered stopping and throwing myself down like a little kid who wasn't being allowed to take home the bag of candy she wanted. But I didn't. Instead, I felt a great weight pressing down around me—responsibility.

For some twisted reason, the universe was bound and determined to see me shoulder some responsibility.

"Fine," I snapped.

"Captain on deck," someone said when we walked onto the command deck.

I noticed that most people didn't turn around and give me a sharp salute or anything, and Miles had to literally push me onto the captain's dais.

"Issue the order to destroy the *Justus*," Miles said.

I turned and stared at him. "You want me to order all of those people to their deaths?"

"Do you think they wouldn't do the same if the situation was reversed?" Miles asked.

I shook my head. "If I'm going to be captain, then

I make the decisions. Not you or anyone else. And I won't be responsible for the deaths of hundreds of people."

"Then be prepared to run for the rest of your short life," Miles said.

"So be it." I wasn't going to become that person. I wasn't going to become my father, who choose to kill in order to solve a problem. Another solution had to be available.

[The ship's targeting systems are capable of destroying the Justus's jump drive's outer-shell components.]

I let out a long sigh of relief. *Thanks, Sam. Do it.*

"Sir, the ship is targeting the *Justus*," someone behind me said.

Miles gave me a grin and turned. "On screen," he ordered.

The image of the *Justus* took front and center. We all watched as our targeting lasers activated, then a small hide-and-seek missile launched.

"That's it?" Miles asked, highly irritated.

"Yup. Now, get us out of here. And that's an order," I said to the crew.

"Yes, sir."

The screen went dark as the missile exploded, and bits of debris circled the *Justus*. I felt the faintest hint of a shift in movement as the *Samaritan* brought its own powerful jump drives on line.

I turned to Miles. "Now. That's finished. Take me to Cain."

Miles gave me a disapproving look but turned and kept his end of the deal.

I shivered as we entered the medical bay. The memories of being held in a nearly identical room by Mrs. Gol were resurfacing. But when I spotted Cain, I could think of nothing else.

Medical personnel were scurrying back and forth, working to mend more than just my IGJ agent. I rushed past them and had to restrain an impulse to throw myself at him.

I looked over at Miles. "I thought you said he was okay."

Miles shook his head. "I never said those exact words. I told you he would survive as long as you did your part. And you did. You got us out of here. Now—" Miles looked down at Cain. "The rest is up to him. More or less."

"What does that mean?" I laid a hand against the medical field protecting Cain's body, hoping his eyes would flutter open. "He talked to me," I whispered. *<Cain? Where are you?>*

I could feel the hint of his presence, a mere fraction of what it normally felt like, and for some reason, that terrified me more than when his presence had been gone.

"Doctor Ashter?" Miles asked.

I didn't even whip around to make sure it was the famous Dr. Ashter, nor did I feel much relief at knowing he'd survived the ordeal with the IGJ.

"Mr. Suren ed-Turen is in a deep coma. When we brought him on board the *Samaritan*, he was conscious, and I had hoped it was a sign he was on the mend... or at least present enough to be able to receive medical attention. For right now, all we can do is keep him stable and hope he'll wake again. I need him conscious to give him a silithium dioric injection."

"I don't understand. What do you mean?" I asked.

"The physical trauma inflicted upon him was brutal enough, but it was the mental trauma that is causing so much damage. I presume she's his heart's blood?"

I lifted my eyes at the question, and Miles nodded in response.

"What business is it of yours?" I snapped.

"Every bit, if you wish to see him returned to health. It would appear the IGJ injected him with a crude form of loprizamine, the drug used to sever the telepathic link between heart's blood," Dr. Ashter said.

"Why would anyone do that?"

Dr. Ashter gave a rather annoyed sigh.

But Miles was the one who spoke. "Tell her."

"Tell me what?" I turned to face both men.

"I can see you're not familiar with Dar physiology," Dr. Ashter started.

"Don't insult me. Tell me what's going on," I said. I'd deactivated the death hook and dropped it into one of my pockets when I ran to the transfer hub. My hand moved to touch that pocket, and for an instant, I considered using the weapon as an incentive.

Miles moved to my side and grabbed my wrist to stop me.

"Don't tell me you're telepathic too, now." I glared at him.

Miles shook his head. "No, just a fairly good judge of humanity. You're tired and overwhelmed. And as you've proven, you aren't the type of person to kill to get what you need. I might not agree with it or even think it's wise, but I'll do what Cain would wish. He would stop you, and so will I."

I don't know the reasons for what happened next, maybe the culmination of the past events, which had been so overwhelming and emotionally draining and crammed into an unbelievably short period, or maybe the fact that Miles was one step ahead of me again. I chalked it up to emotional and physical exhaustion.

But my whole body sagged, and Miles reached out and caught me, and I leaned against the madman for support.

"Just tell me, please," I said to Dr. Ashter.

"Heart's blood connections are rare and considered a throwback to an earlier time in Darquet evolution. But with the mixing of genetics from other species, there have been interesting... ramifications, one of which is the heart's blood connection with someone not of Darquet ancestry. Unless you think you might have a Darquet ancestor somewhere, then that would change things a little."

He gave me an inquisitive look, but I shook my head. I was one hundred percent, pure-grade human, or at least I was pretty sure I was.

"Dar boasts one of the harshest justice systems in the known worlds," Dr. Ashter continued. "In the rare case of an individual who has made a heart's blood connection, and they've committed a level three offense, loprizamine will be administered to the offender. This drug effectively shuts down the heart's blood connection. I only know of two cases where it was rumored to be reversed to full strength. Silithium dioric will help repair some damaged neurons and areas of the brain involved in this ability but not completely. For that… well…" He glanced at Miles.

Miles was the one who said, "It's believed you need the family's heart stone to completely repair the connection."

The information swirled around inside me until it eventually settled down and I could connect the dots. "Wait. That doesn't make sense. Cain talked to me on the *Justus* when everything went sideways. How could they have severed the link if he was still able to communicate with me?"

Dr. Ashter and Miles exchanged a look I didn't care for. "Tell me."

"If Mr. Suren ed-Turen did indeed telepathically communicate with you after the injection, then it would account for the amount of neurological damage we're seeing," Dr. Ashter said.

I bit my lip and turned my head to try to hide my tears. *<You foolish man.>*

"Is there anything else, Dr. Ashter?" Miles asked.

"We're working to repair the physical damage although we won't be able to regenerate or grow a clone tail for Mr. Suren ed-Turen without his consent. I am hopeful once the physical damage is taken care of, he will regain consciousness. I'll keep you informed."

"Thank you," I whispered and let Miles lead me toward the door.

One of the attendants rushed up to us. "Sir, we have an incoming message for a Mahia Orion."

"Put it up on a screen," Miles said.

I let go of him, took a deep breath, and tried to straighten myself up as best I could. I needn't have bothered as the message wasn't live. But I felt a surge of rage as the screen flickered to life, and the image of Commandant Yilmaz filled the screen.

"Congratulations on surviving the first round," she said. "I wonder how you will fare the next time we'll need to set up a meeting." She leaned back and winced visibly. Her hand reached up and touched a dark patch of skin on the side of her neck. "You'll need to mark your calendar because it won't be long until I find you. The IGJ has upgraded your status and that of your friends to the Most Wanted section. This means every bounty hunter, every agent, and every individual will know your faces and be on the lookout. I wish you well in trying to evade me for too long."

Yilmaz paused and looked off-screen for a moment before turning her focus back to the message. "You should have killed me when you had the chance. I know your father would have. Perhaps you should take a few pointers from him after all."

The screen went dark, and all I could feel was rage—at Yilmaz, at my father, at the whole tangled mess. I whirled around and ran. No one tried to stop me as I ran through the decks. Not having any particular destination in mind, I only needed to move. And when I'd exhausted myself, I collapsed in the corridor.

Either Miles had ordered the ship's personnel to stay away and give me space, or I'd found a part of the ship that wasn't heavily trafficked. Either way, I didn't care. I let the cool touch of the ship's metallic walls seep through my jumpsuit and into my skin.

When Cain and I had been discussing what to do after the events aboard the *Rapscallion*, I hadn't been ready to confront what my father had done or what he was possibly a part of. But I was ready right then. Everyone seemed to be holding more cards in their hands than I did, but I was ready to enter the game, to bet the whole enchilada.

But I had one thing to attend to first.

Cain.

I needed to do everything in my power to make sure he had the chance to heal and see our connection restored. Besides, we'd had a sort of deal. I would help him figure out Project Clear Sight and boost his ranking, then we would go and help his sister.

Well, the ranking boost he'd hoped for wasn't going to come. I hoped he wouldn't be too terribly disappointed over that one. In fact, I was quite sure that Cain was no longer an IGJ agent at all, not if he was on their Most Wanted list. *Whoops.*

But we would go to Dar, and I would get Cain the help he needed, and we would free his sister. Then Yilmaz and everyone else had better watch out because Mahia Orion was coming for them.

31

Scratch That…
Redrawing the Lines

After I'd cooled down, found an empty hab-unit, and slept for more than two shift rotations, I cleaned myself up, got some food, checked on Cain, and made my way up to the command deck. My mind was clear, and a few things needed to be taken care of.

Miles was there, sitting comfortably in the captain's chair, reading through what I presumed was a report.

"Captain on deck," one of the officers said.

Miles turned and threw me a grin. "Feeling better now?"

I nodded. "Much. Update."

He raised an eyebrow and chuckled. "Feeling like you're in control, huh?"

"I'm the captain, after all," I said, "and you're sitting in my chair."

Miles bounced up, and with a flourish, he bowed, "Oh, pardon me, oh great captain, my captain."

"Cut it out and just give me an update," I said as I eyed the chair.

I wasn't really going to be the captain, and when I stepped onto the command deck, I'd had every intention of telling Sam to transfer it to someone else. But seeing Miles in the chair had given me a twinge of irritation. The change in command could wait for a moment longer.

"We're three weeks out from Dar," Miles said. "No signs of pursuit. We crippled the *Justus* pretty well. I'm guessing they'll need a tow barge to pull them into a repair dock on Lunar 5."

"Three weeks is a long time," I murmured.

Miles nodded in a brief moment of genuine empathy. "Cain will survive. Give him time. The IGJ did a number on him, but he'll make it. Plus, we'll need the time to get the both of you ready."

"Ready?"

Miles shook his head. "Do you think you're going to be able to walk into any transfer hub looking the way you do? They've shut down all non-Darquet traveling to the planet. You're going to have to spend some time under the bright lights of genetic modeling." His face split into a wide grin while mine dropped into a deep frown. "You're going to look stunning as a Darquet."

I knew some people messed around with genetic modeling, temporary restructuring of the physical body to match a different species. But mostly, I'd chalked it up as a thing of jute-store novels, maybe government spies or the like. But it wasn't something that was common practice.

"And what about bioscans?" I asked.

"Oh, we'll take care of that too. Don't worry," Miles said.

Oh, but I did, especially with that twinkle in his eye. Miles might not have been quite as crazy as I first thought he was, but that didn't mean I trusted him—or thought he wouldn't do something for a laugh at the expense of me or Cain. The only thing I did feel sure about was that he didn't want us dead, at least not at the moment.

I narrowed my eyes and looked at Miles suspiciously. "Why are you being so helpful?"

Miles shrugged. "We need the time to regroup. Figure out the next steps in the larger scheme of things. And I need you fully focused on what's going on. I'm assuming that won't happen until your precious former IGJ agent is all healed up, correct?"

I nodded. "But what makes you think I'm going to help you? Or get tangled up any further in this mess?"

Miles threw me a wild grin and cocked his head to the side "Aren't you?"

I gave him a harrumph and crossed my arms against my chest. "Annoying know-it-all. But I've still got a bone to pick with you. Don't think I've forgotten about your little sleight of hand with the smart bots."

Miles sighed. "In time. All in due time."

"No," I said and dropped the lighthearted demeanor. "You'll tell me now, or I'll have you thrown into the brig."

Evidently, my change in attitude was sharp enough to catch his attention. "You're not ready."

"That's my choice to make, not yours. You'll tell me

what you intended with the smart bots, or else you can spend some time in a dark hole. Your choice."

Miles tilted his head to one side and stared at me. "No."

"Choice made, then. Lock him up."

He grinned. "And who's going to do that? You?"

I eyed the chair and sat down. "I am the captain, after all. And I've given a direct order. Miles High is to be arrested and thrown into the brig."

The grin faded, and for a moment, Miles looked outraged. As two officers moved forward to follow orders, Miles sniffed. "Fine. A little solitude never hurt anyone."

I leaned back into the chair and considered what was awaiting me. Never in a million light-years would I have guessed my life would take such a drastic turn. And in that second, I didn't know the half of it.

"We have an incoming message. No, wait," someone behind us said.

I twisted in the chair and took note of a flurry of activity taking place.

"Can you confirm that?" a woman asked another officer.

"Hang on... yes. Message confirmed. We're receiving multiple messages now," the officer replied.

"Sir, the news feeds are jammed with flash updates," another called out.

Miles straightened, and together, we asked, "What's the message?" which annoyed me to no end.

"Sirs, Lunar 5... It's—"

"Spit it out," Miles said.

"It's gone."

Talk about your drastic turns.

"Excuse me?" I said.

"On screen," Miles snapped.

The screen lit up to show… nothing. Well, not nothing. Chunks of debris were floating there, from the moon and the ships and the infrastructure.

"That can't… there's no way," I said then snapped my mouth shut. "Surely, this is a joke. How can the whole moon be gone?"

Miles didn't say anything but plopped down to the floor and stared at the screen. My little order to arrest him was temporarily forgotten in the chaos.

My brain couldn't handle what the officers were trying to tell me, all giving me different reports and different angles on what was being broadcast. That type of thing just didn't happen. Sure, catastrophic accidents occurred on ships and stations and even planetside. Wars and battles took a heavy toll as well. Certain moons and a few planets had become permanently uninhabitable during the Cricade Wars. But I couldn't ever recall a historic event where a moon or anything had been completely destroyed.

"Was there a malfunction within the base? Some kind of horrific chain reaction that could've done this?" I asked.

"No, sir. From what we know of Lunar 5, there was nothing there that would have had the destructive capacity to destroy the moon. Even in a full system-wide meltdown across the different zones on the base," one of the officers answered.

I looked down. "Miles?"

He just sat there and shook his head.

"Are there any survivors?" I asked.

"We're getting conflicting reports, but I don't think so, sir. Whatever happened was instantaneous and caused resulting chain reactions in any ships or structures within the blast radius."

"Sirs, we've got another incoming message," someone informed us.

"Turn them off and begin consolidating informa-tion," Miles said as he pushed himself off. "With what-ever or whoever did this, I don't want to stand around and be another piece of target practice."

"Sir, it isn't related to Lunar 5. It's a message for direct communication from another ship. But I can't seem to get a fix on its location," the officer said.

"Auditory only," Miles said and looked at me. "We don't need to broadcast exactly who we are just yet."

"Auditory only. Yes, sir," the officer said.

After a pause, I heard a crackle and a voice I hadn't thought I would ever hear again.

"Hey, sis. How's it going?"

"Lucas?" I said and stood, my mouth hanging open.

"You got it in one. I see you've kicked quite the hor-net's nest with the IGJ and all. Didn't think you had it in you," Lucas replied.

"How… What are you doing here?" I asked.

"Oh, lending a hand. I had thought about destroying the *Justus* for you but then thought better. Having Yilmaz around will help keep you on your toes for a while. But I've got a new toy to play with and thought, hell, why not give it a try with Lunar 5? It's not that important in the grand scheme of things. And now everyone's going to be wondering what's going on. Keeps the masses off-balance, maybe kick-starts a new war. Anything to keep people off the trail of the real prize."

"You did this?" I asked in shock.

"Nifty, eh? Maybe the Jumjul and others will think twice before messing around with us now. Let humanity take the reins," Lucas said. "Anyway, just wanted to check in with you. I know it's been a while. We've got a lot of catching up to do, but that'll have to wait for another time. Oh, and say hello to your agent for me, will you? You've hooked an interesting one, I'll give you that. You do what you need to do. Take your time. But when you're ready, I'm here. And I won't jerk you around like Yilmaz did. I'll give you the answers you want. But only when you're ready, and you'll know when that is."

What do you say when you hear from a brother you haven't had contact with in years, who abruptly reveals himself while proudly announcing he's literally blown up a moon?

Nothing—that was what I said. I stood there in shock.

"Sir, end of transmission. Orders?"

"Get us the hell out of here," I said then turned to face Miles. "We've got a lot to talk about."

No joking, no hint of anything but a dead-serious expression was etched on his face. And fear. I could see it in his eyes, in the way he held his mouth—all new expressions from the ex-monarch.

"Sir, new message. This one is on a wide broadcast."

"On screen," I said.

The screen flared to life once more, and the image of my brother filled the screen. He looked the same yet different. I could see a bit of our father in there, but at the same time, a complete stranger was staring at me—not directly at me, just into the camera when he recorded the message.

"My name is Lucas Orion, and I'm here today to tell you there's a new dawn on the horizon for humanity, one where we take our next steps into our rightful inheritance. What you've witnessed with Lunar 5 is but a small taste of what we're capable of. For now, be mindful of the shadows and watch the darkened corners, because we're watching, and we're preparing. The glory of the new dawn is almost upon us."

Lucas's face disappeared and was replaced by a symbol, the image that had been tattooed on Mrs. Gol's shoulder, the image my father had also carried on his body.

It was the simple outline of a sun.

Thank you for reading *Project Clear Sight*!

Don't miss out on what happens next for Mahia and Cain or explore what other titles I have to offer. You can sign-up to stay in touch through my newsletter at:

elizabethknollston.com

You can also follow me on social media at:
facebook.com/elizabethknollston
twitter.com/EKnollston

Look for the third installment of the
The Three-Fold Suns Series

The Diplomats of Dar

and discover the twists and turns that are on the horizon!

Acknowledgements

It's a little crazy to realize that my lifelong dream of being an author is coming true. A dream which would never have become reality if not for the support of so many family members and friends. I will always thank my parents first. Without their encouragement of exploring the secrets, mysteries, and adventures contained within a book, I wouldn't be where I'm today.

To all of my family and friends who've supported me, all I can say is a huge thank you. Especially to my aunts and uncles, who mean so much to me. Your endless cheerleading and wise counsel have helped give me the confidence to step into the wild worlds of being a self-published author. Thank you so much for believing in me!

A huge shout out to Katie, who has been reading the stories as they've been written, and letting me sound off ideas. I've appreciated all of your generous help and support!

And of course, I couldn't have gotten this book to where it is today without the editors at Red Adept Editing. A huge thank you for all the hard work which they've done in order to help polish this story!

Thank you, everyone for encouraging me and believing in me! Thank you, readers for taking a chance on this book and I look forward to writing more fantastical and intergalactic adventures!

About the Author

Elizabeth Knollston collects dragons. No, they're not real. But if you know of a mad scientist or genetic engineer who's working on the real deal, be sure to let her know. She would dearly love to collect star ships too, but those won't fit in her garage.

Her (overactive) imagination is credit to her parents, who outrageously encouraged her poor spending habits of buying too many books. And just a side note—if you ever plan on moving, book collecting isn't helpful.

In another life, Elizabeth dreamed of becoming an archaeologist, but a fascinating and rewarding job as a therapeutic horseback riding instructor derailed those plans. When Elizabeth isn't wondering about being on a manned mission to Mars, she enjoys bugging her dog, battling the weeds in her garden, and being a productive member of society.